DYING TIMES

DYING TIMES

Darlene Madott

Library and Archives Canada Cataloguing in Publication

Title: Dying times / Darlene Madott.
Names: Madott, Darlene, author.
Identifiers: Canadiana (print) 20210232889 | Canadiana (ebook) 20210232927 |
ISBN 9781550969498 (hardcover) | ISBN 9781550969504 (EPUB) |
ISBN 9781550969511 (Kindle) | ISBN 9781550969528 (PDF)
Classification: LCC PS8576.A335 D95 2021 | DDC C813/.54—dc23

Copyright © Darlene Madott, 2021
Text and cover design by Michael Callaghan
Cover painting "Ante Litem Motam" by Francesca Trop
The poem *Small Miracles* © Joyce Carol Oates, from the book *Aurora, New Canadian
Writing 1978*, edited by Morris Wolfe, Doubleday Canada Limited, Toronto, 1978
Typeset in Granjon font at Moons of Jupiter Studios
Published by Exile Editions Ltd ~ www.ExileEditions.com
144483 Southgate Road 14 – GD, Holstein, Ontario, N0G 2A0
Printed and Bound in Canada by Marquis

We gratefully acknowledge the Canada Council for the Arts, the Government of
Canada, the Ontario Arts Council, and Ontario Creates for their support
toward our publishing activities.

Canadian sales representation: The Canadian Manda Group, 664 Annette Street,
Toronto ON M6S 2C8 www.mandagroup.com 416 516 0911

North American and international distribution, and U.S. sales:
Independent Publishers Group, 814 North Franklin Street,
Chicago IL 60610 www.ipgbook.com toll free: 1 800 888 4741

*With thanks
to Barry Callaghan for freeing the voice,
for giving so generously of his talent and time
– and to all the Jacks of this world,
who say it straight.*

DYING TIMES

Blessed are they that mourn;
For they shall be comforted.
—MATTHEW 5:4

Blessed are they that hunger
And thirst after justice, for they
Shall have their fill.
—MATTHEW 5:6

My mother is dying. My senior law partner, Jack, is dying. Our richest client, Bernie Spurling, is dying – each taking their own sweet time, defying predictions. They say my mother has maybe three weeks to live. She is not dying fast enough for Jack. He says he needs me to interview witnesses and wants Bernie's trial fast-tracked to happen before the first day of spring. He says this is because he's got maybe six months to live. Bernie, our quadriplegic client confined to a wheelchair, wants his case done and gone before his wife can get her hands on his money. "Not one fucking cent."

I am taking their deaths into me. There's no way out of any of this. I am the goldfish in the bowl in my childhood home; the fish flashed over glittering blue crystals we didn't know were lethal. My mother had bought these crystals at the dollar store, thinking they would liven up the goldfish's confined universe. The fish flailed about. I thought it was all play until I understood it to be fish language for dying. Dying had been the fight of its life.

Liar

Talk with the palliative care doctor has gone off the rails.

The palliative care doctor had said, "Your mother is getting enough morphine to tank an elephant." Yet, when he asked her if it hurt *here*, and then *here*, she said "yes" to everything. Even the soft tissue. Everything hurt – but with a smile. Mom's smile: her warm, forgiving, beatific smile which, of course, he didn't recognize or comprehend.

"The pain, it must be psychological," the doctor said, trying for thoughtfulness.

"I'll tell you where the pain comes from," I said, pointing at my angry older sister. "Our mother's fervent wish, when she moved in here, was to finally be free from her eldest daughter and her son-in-law."

"Get out of my face, get out," Elizabeth sputtered. Louie, her husband, pointed at me, crying, "You need to know, she's an aggressive litigator, a liar." Instinctively, the doctor took hold of my mother's hand, as if he might protect her from her children.

"Whatever the unfortunate history of your family," the doctor said, "you all need to let your mother die in peace."

My mother had told me the pain was like "dogs gnawing at my bones," or "something taking hold of a leg or finger bone, and slowly twisting it around and around under the skin." On top of being driven to tears by the excruciating pain of bone marrow cancer, Mom now asked me if she was going nuts, if this was all in her head? "Not even the doctor believes me."

"I believe you, Mom."

"I feel horrible. You have no idea how horrible this feels. I hope to God you never know."

Senior Partner's Shtetel Wisdom

"Too smart is half a fool."

Bernie Spurling was describing his wife, "She gets herself a little bit of knowledge, and she thinks she's an expert.

Pretty soon she'll even believe in her own lies. She makes herself into a very convincing liar."

Jack assured him: "Bernie, over 50 years, I've made a living out of liars. Your soon-to-be-former wife hates me now. Wait till I cross-examine her. She'll like me even less." Jack was pleased with himself. His face had gone from chemo ashen to sunburnt pink at the prospect of cross-examining Bernie's wife.

Jack had told me that Bernie's divorce was a "career file." He meant the kind of big-buck case that comes once in a lifetime and either makes or breaks a lawyer's career.

Of the client Jack said: "His condition is awful: Mine is just that I'm dying."

The Family Law Act, 1985

More than three decades earlier, I had been in the first years of my practice. Jack had taken me under his wing. I had gotten into an argument with one of the firm's partners; a blue suit, stuffed shirt who'd decided to cross-examine me because I'd asked for a second filing cabinet. I needed more room for my own burgeoning practice. The partner didn't believe I had that many active files. So I hauled open each drawer of my single cabinet. "Active file, active, active, active," slamming each drawer shut, opening the next.

When I told my father about the firm's abusive male lawyers (I was the only female among 10 angry men) my father said: "You face your dragons where you find them. Change firms, and it will just be the same dragon but with a different face." My father had been an artist, a painter, who supported us through his lettering business: United Signs and Outdoor Advertising. He'd been a good painter in oils on canvas and a surprisingly good businessman for an artist. About the cabinets, Jack said to me: "Why didn't you come to me?"

"Because you're not my father. I have to slay my own dragons." Jack liked what he called the fire in my belly, my creativity, my independence.

From that point on, I had a history with Jack. Our professional intimacy began, I guess, with a couple called the Divots.

Mr. and Mrs. Divot were odd ducks. Their case was one of the first under the new *Family Law Act* and my first case working alongside Jack. The act had shifted the focus from family assets and non-family assets to marriage as a partnership. The new law equalized the growth in properties as between the husband and wife from the value assessed on the date of the marriage to the date of separation. In the Divot case, oddly, there was no equalization payment owing from one to the other. Neither Jack nor I could figure how it was possible to organize a marriage this way, with equal piles of nickels and dimes on both sides of the ledger.

Mrs. Divot had chosen to leave Mr. Divot for one simple reason. She realized that after his mother's death they were not going to inherit anything close to the millions she'd expected. Mrs. Divot – to make it clear that she was angry and done with the family – took a Sunday carving knife and slashed an ancestral Divot portrait. I had to rush to court the next morning to slap a lien against the matrimonial home, title to which had only just been conveyed to Mrs. Divot's name.

As we approached trial, Jack – who was actually disgusted by the players in the case, hating their pettiness, their vindictiveness – tried to wiggle out of the retainer. (Jack himself totalled three wives over the course of his life, but he left everything he owned at the time of separation to each in succession. *"Things,"* he said, *"never defined me."* I thought his generosity toward his wives was what made him work to the grave. But dying while in harness was also a badge of honour. *"You see this desk,"* Jack proclaimed proudly. *"This desk converts into a coffin."*)

When husband Divot came up with the $50,000 retainer on the eve of trial, Jack and I were stuck with the Divots.

Eager junior-lawyer-me went to work. I placed the trial binder in Jack's hands: opening statement, scripted examination-in-chief, cross-examination of Mrs. Divot, summaries of the discovery transcripts, law section as to the evidentiary and substantive issues, closing argument. Jack looked up from his wingback chair. He was chewing relentlessly on his toothbrush. He asked what the firm paid me and raised me 10, like he was playing poker.

At the courthouse the next morning, I straightened Jack's white tabs, which were lopsided and unruly at the neck of his black silk robe.

Because of that, I ran into a new kind of hostility, much more wounding than macho bruising over filing cabinets. Our opposing female counsel, a declared feminist, scolded me at the break. "You behave like an abused woman." She was talking about how I had handled Jack's tabs. Tabs!

I told her flat out – how brilliant Jack was, what a privilege it was to work with him, how much I learned from him.

"I rest my case," said the female counsel. "Abused people always defend their abusers and find reasons to forgive and forget. What about his tabs? Can't he adjust those for himself in a mirror?"

Is sanctimony – righteous sanctimony – preferable to an over-weaning sense of macho-self just because it is in stiletto heels? Accessorized by a strategic slit in the skirt? I'll say it straight, we were in a winners' game, and Jack and I played to win. Anything less was, and would be, a disservice to our clients. Mrs. Divot's counsel, mouthing superior all the way, was about to lose. Which meant Mrs. Divot – not counsel – would pay for the loss.

So, of course, Jack was hard-nosed. He'd take you for lunch and have you for lunch. From time to time, I tried to call Jack on this kind of behaviour. I even tried as we worked our way through the Bernie case.

"Jack, we have to talk."

"We don't have to talk."

"Jack, I have opinions. A mind of my own. I can't go back to being the junior lawyer and handmaiden I once was. I can't just follow obediently."

"Whatever I do, I do to protect you. You're on a need-to-know basis. You don't have to understand the whole of it."

That was it.

He had a hard mouth. Direct, demanding, all too often, utterly insensitive. He abused men and women alike.

Me, included. But damn it, he was good, sometimes great at what he did. He knew what he knew. He knew a lot. Sometimes he didn't know what he didn't know. And that would cause a hitch in what we were doing. But he was no fool. A hitch isn't a halt. Best of all, he was never fooled by fools. By sentimentality, never. By sanctimony, never.

They used to say about such men: He's tough. He's a straight shooter. Well, Jack was a tough lawyer who was dying; he was a dead man walking. I couldn't say to him: *"Dying is no license to abuse. You can't just beat on people like you do so you can get your way. You've no idea what it does to those who love you, who'll survive you."*

I consoled myself by saying that to myself. Not to a dying man from whom I'd learned almost everything about life and law. Now, I'm learning about dying.

At the end of the Divot case, just as with every case we fought together over the years, Jack gave me some of his *shtetel* wisdom: "Humans can get used to anything – even Auschwitz."

One case became another. Different faces. Different facts. Different lies. Same betrayals. Same greed. Same hate. In the end, they all blended together, like dust. *Will we make it to the end of the Bernie case,* I wondered. *Will we fight this last one together?*

Jack gave me his *shtetel* wisdom. I wanted to give Jack something:

"I told my mother about you. She says she would gladly give you what's left of her days."

Jack was shocked. Speechless. And I'd thought nothing could surprise him.

Whatever Has a Beginning Must Have an End

About the big bang theory. It wasn't known about back when I was born. In Sunday school, we were told that God is infinite and that infinity means *no beginning and no end*. At the age of five, trying to contemplate what *no beginning* was, had brought on night terrors. I could somehow cope with the idea of no end, but that something could have no beginning…? What about me? My mother and father? What did my beginning mean if we had no beginning? During the night terrors, I'd sleep run, not sleepwalk, around our apartment above my father's sign shop until Dad would catch me up in his arms and make me drink a glass of water.

This was the dream that had me running barefoot in my seersucker pyjamas:

I am in some kind of very constricted, snake-like tunnel, crawling slowly toward its end, toward the light. Just as I get there, someone plugs up that end of the tunnel and I am trapped in darkness forever.

I am told that, in fact, the umbilical cord had been roped around my neck at birth. It was a miracle I survived. I have been told that I am one of the lucky ones: delivered from my own darkness alive.

Swimming

Water is my element, born under the sign of Pisces. I have never been afraid of water. I remember floating as a child in maybe a foot of water close to the shore of Ossossane Beach so my mother could see me floating free and easy, my mother seated on her beach towel, flipping through celebrity magazines. Along with my baby sister, Rose, and older sister, Elizabeth, they all feared water. Eventually, my mother would have to force me out of the lake, out of the water, at around noon so she could comb and braid my hair. My lips would be blue from hours of swimming.

Since it was obvious that I was at ease in the water and as I grew, it was important to my mother that I take serious swimming and diving lessons. I readily passed through all the aquatic levels, achieving a bronze certification. My only difficulty was with the 10-foot dive to the bottom of a pool, to retrieve a puck. A puck! (There's always something crazy and elusive about life. In diving, it was the puck.) But staying on the surface was no problem. I could tread water, endlessly, and each summer I'd swim across the bay and back to where Dad had built a cottage for us on Clear Lake in Haliburton. As time passed, Mom wanted to learn how to swim, too, so as a teenager, I got it into my head to teach my mother how to swim. But I had to *overcome her fear.* Her fear of going under.

I suited us up with life jackets – flinging myself from a raft so she'd see that it is impossible to sink in a life jacket. Then, we went into the lake together, she in her life jacket, me holding her by the hand, until she got, gradually, the sensation of floating.

But in a sudden welling of panic, she realized that she'd lost any feel for the bottom. Mom grabbed me, pressing me under the water, smothering me with her life jacket. I'd been told what to do when a drowning person clings to you, drowning you, too. I kicked her in the gut. Freed, I flipped her onto her back, face away from me, and with one hand under her back, lifted her toward the sky. In her red jacket, she looked like an overturned ladybug, drifting on the current. I had strong, long legs. I kicked us back to shore.

"She called me an Effing Cripple"

Bernie Spurling's penthouse condo was all rainbows, swimming in light through the cut crystals of the antique collection he'd managed to rescue from the matrimonial mansion.

"She thought I'd be afraid, called me an effing cripple, in front of my children. She thought I'd never have the guts to leave her, the effing bottom-feeding bitch. I've never been so happy. The legal fees. Every bit of it. All worth it – to escape."

On the other side of fear lies freedom. It's about overcoming the fear. That, or having no other choice.

More Shtetel Wisdom

"You don't shit where you eat."

Back at the beginning of my legal career, trial preparation had always started with Jack cooking a meal. For the Divot case, Jack made me chopped liver sandwiches served up with bacon and onions on toasted rye and topped by deli ketchup. I have never tasted a more delicious breakfast.

By the time of the Bernie Spurling case, Jack's meals had become more sophisticated. Preparing for Bernie was poached salmon and leeks.

We worked all day, side-by-side. But one evening, in his condo, Jack went missing. I found him dead to the world, sprawled on his bed in his silk housecoat, sleeping.

Was he really sleeping, or was the open door some kind of test?

At 10 o'clock that night, I tiptoed out of Jack's condo, having arranged and packed all our briefs for the next day, leaving the door unlocked behind me.

The next morning, Jack said nothing about my departure, nothing about the unlocked door.

Jack is not an ordinary man. He cannot be judged by everyday standards. I have always thought, if there is a God, then God must be something like Jack – an engaged enough sinner to understand, a profound enough saint to forgive. It has been, and still is a privilege to serve such a man, even if it involves adjusting his tabs or *schlepping* his law briefs.

There is another reason I cannot abandon this dying man.

Fear

"Mom, why did you write down that you refuse everything, in advance – feeding tubes, intravenous, oxygen – while at the same time you said 'yes' to transfusions… *'for now'*… after all the doctor told you that the transfusions were extending your life, but also extending your pain? I don't get it."

We're in the hospital transfusion room. The Voyageur transportation paramedics are waiting in another room. Mom's hematologist, Dr. Arlene Shaw, is waiting for an answer. My older sister Elizabeth, and her doting dumb-mouthed husband, Louie, are waiting, too. For Mom to change her mind, to refuse the blood. Period. I show the doctor the paper Mom had signed, with me as witness, where she had gone so far as to say that she no longer wanted to continue the blood transfusions, adding, *for now.*

"I can override this," Dr. Shaw says.

"It's okay, Mom, you take all the time you need," I say. Dr. Shaw is waiting to see if Mom's refusal is tentative or not. She is impatient.

Elizabeth, as if there were no confusion, asks if she should take Mom for her scheduled blood test.

"What would be the point," Dr. Shaw offers, "to inflict unnecessary pain?"

To Elizabeth's fury (any frustration or change in plans brings on her fury), Mom reiterates that she is refusing any transfusion, *for now*. I say, "Okay, then I will see her back to her room in the retirement home."

The November day is spectacular, full of brilliant sunshine. On the ride back from the hospital to Mountain Vista Village with the Voyageur transport paramedics, the bare black branches flash shadows as we pass. In Mom's room, I again ask why?

"Why *for now*, and then you're going to change your mind?"

"I'm afraid," Mom says flatly.

I consider the decision she has made this day, how huge it was, how huge it must be to refuse all further treatment, even tentatively, tantalizingly holding onto or out for hope.

"You are the most courageous woman I know."

"I don't know about that," Mom says with a wan smile. "No, I don't."

You should not cry when you are on your last journey
   —Jewish Resistance Song, 1943 in the Vilna Ghetto

Jack, my senior partner, has told me these words. Later, he adjusts the words:
   "Never say that you are on your last journey."

Pumpkins on the Ridge

A year ago, visiting Mom at her Martin Grove condo: Believing that she's had enough of her four walls, I take her out, not appreciating – no matter her eagerness – how hard it is for her to get ready, then having to wait in her coat near the door. I think I have found the perfect formula for a perfect day – to spend most of it just driving around, as I'd once had to drive my sleepless infant son, Marco.

   Getting her down to the parked car, the hazards flashing at the condo door, the seat warmers pre-heating the leather, lattes in the holders, I ease her into the front, fasten the seat belts and head north up highway 427. We stop at an all-day breakfast place, eat, and then drive on. Though we've just eaten, I suggest we stop somewhere for ice cream. She expresses her surprise, since she knows I don't particularly like ice cream, not since I was a kid. She doesn't know my dislike comes not because of taste, but from a determined resistance to my sister Elizabeth, who had called me "fatso" after I'd eaten almost a bucketful of ice cream as a kid.

Staring out the car window together at the passing farms prompts stories of her childhood, when she ran with her arms outstretched through the wheatfield adjoining the family's rented farmland outside the city, her father throwing his Sicilian peasant hat up into the air at the spring rain: "goodbye *cappucia*," joyous in his expectation of the growing cabbages to come. And memories, too, of her own mother, coming from the city on weekends, after a working week at Cook's Clothing down on Front Street, Toronto, to make rabbit *cacciatore* on an outdoor stove.

In my car, Mom sleeps a blessed hour, a rest she can never achieve in the lonely condo hours of "staring at the four walls" she hates, that she had acceded to within a year of Dad's death, under Elizabeth's influence, having agreed to move from her big house on Veneto Drive to the isolation of the Martin Grove condo. Her life, after Dad's death, had become an excruciating exercise, waiting in bewildering pain, swirling through thoughts of obedience, disobedience, anger. "Why won't God take me?" This before any of us knew about the acute bone marrow cancer. Later, she'd question the pain, and ultimately, she questioned God. "I don't think I was a bad person. I don't think I ever hurt anyone." In truth, she had travelled through life as an unassuming woman, trailing little or no harm. Tempted in the condo by suicide, thinking she might pull a chair close to the balcony and throw herself over – this she also denied herself, lest she hurt *anyone else* by falling on them.

The journey north in the car is a Halloween Sunday. I stop at a display of pumpkins. I buy three. The figure quoted by the boy who is selling them is seven dollars apiece. I ask him if he will give me three for twenty dollars, and he tells me that a man asked him that very same question, only this morning. I learn from his proud mother that he has just started Grade Five and that the boy had struck a bargain with his mother and father – they'd let him have his own pumpkin plot if he would tend to the seedlings, grow them, and sell them, and keep the money made for his education fund. The boy proudly carries the pumpkins to my car. My mother watches from the open window. The boy's little sister has been neglected in our conversation. Mom has always had an eye for the meek. She beckons the little girl to the car window and finds something to praise about her, while I negotiate for three additional gourds, for three dollars and not five.

I toot the horn as we pull onto the road and continue north, and through my rear-view mirror I see the family on the wagon, waving to us.

For half an hour I am speechless.

For weeks I've had the feeling that I'm on a whirligig of death and dying...except whirligigs usually give pleasure, they make people laugh, and I am not laughing, or, maybe I am supposed to laugh at laughter – the crazy contagion of it, happening at the most inappropriate moments – maybe that's the only way to deal with dying.

I am in a rush to get back home, to carve my pumpkins, to set my house up for Halloween. I am frantic because of my own physical confinement – in the car, too long, seated, too long.

"It's getting late."

When we turn to head south, in a field to our west, the setting sun catches a ridge of pumpkins on a hill and sets them ablaze.

"Pumpkins! Oh, look," as if I have never seen a pumpkin before – but not like these, lined up like flaming candles.

My father had seen them – four years ago. "Is there a garden outside?" He had asked, from his hospital room, "Are those pumpkins on the ridge?" He had died in August. I want to believe the pumpkins he had seen were these, waiting for us in our future, the future we had then, in a time when he would not be.

"If Dad were here, I would stop to take a photograph of these pumpkins for him to paint," I say to my mother, as we head back to the city.

She is in no rush to get back. She is disturbed about something. I don't want to know, don't want to start a new conversation, after what I feel was a perfect day. Crazily, I suggest another ice cream. She never says no to anything. I come out of the store with two cones. We eat in the car.

"When you get to where you're going," I say, "promise me you'll find a way to get a message back. I want to know if you're seeing my father again."

"I don't think anyone is waiting for me. Anyway, at the rate I'm going, I could never catch up to him, I'll never find him." I risk a glance. Calmly, angrily, she is licking ice cream, taking all the afternoon time I have to give. It is never enough; it will never be enough.

More

More than the greatest love the world has known
This is the love that I give to you alone
More than the simple words I try to say

I only live to love you more each day.
More than you'll ever know
My arms long to hold you so
My life will be in your keeping
Waking, sleeping, laughing, weeping…
—BOBBY DARIN

Their life in each other's keeping lasted 67 years. Until my father's death, at 87, Mom had never been alone a day in her life. Her attempts to learn – at 87 – how to be a widow, endured three years.

My favourite bedtime story, whether it was Dad tucking us into bed or Mom, was the story of how they met. According to both, it was love at first sight.

Mom had gone to a Toronto dance hall, Sunnyside, with her sister Sofia. The story, however, was about the car ride home. Dad's friend Mario was driving because he owned the car. Giovanni was in the back seat with Francesca. With every turn in the road, Giovanni leaned into Francesca. She felt a shock go through her, a warm thrill. Too shy to speak, they sat in silence.

In Mom's story, Dad called her at 7:30 the next morning. She was so shy, "afraid of my shadow," that she put her sister Sofia on the phone to carry on the conversation. She was only 16.

In Dad's story, it was 9:30 in the morning – 7:30 would not have been respectful. He was 23 and said he thought about such things. He said she must have waited beside the phone for two hours.

War came. Dad enlisted. He was stationed at the Canadian National Exhibition Grounds, in Toronto. Through weeks and months, he didn't contact Francesca. By his story, he didn't want to start something that would have to be broken off. My mother, however, had learned that he was there, and she took his silence as a sign. She was so heartsick with loss that her hair began to fall out. She pined for him, she mourned him.

But they found each other again, and a wartime correspondence ensued; and even a recording of his voice reading a letter to *his beloved, yearning to be with her*, and photographs of Dad training on the mountains out west in Whistler, and more and more letters from the time Dad was stationed in Port Alberni. He never did go overseas. Challenged by the English officers, who were trying to shame enlisted men into signing up for "active duty," one demanded to know: "What will you tell your grandchildren?" My father said, "I *will have* grandchildren."

Francesca and Giovanni married in Toronto during the war.

Immediately following the wedding, on Dad's brief furlough, they went to Niagara Falls for their honeymoon. Mom was gorgeous, and Dad was a champion weightlifter, with the hands of an artist. The newlyweds attracted so much attention that Dad – although he had papers permitting civilian clothing – had to put his uniform back on. "Who's the dame?" a group of sailors taunted. "My wife, *and don't you dare dishonor her with your filthy stares."*

Mom was so shy, such an innocent, she hid behind a bureau on their wedding night.

"I was just playing," she said, when I reminded her of this story.

He was so warm. When he put his arms around me, he was always so warm.

She had been protected throughout the whole of their lives, right to the end. And then, she found herself alone. With no one to prepare a table in the presence of her enemies.

In the beautiful intimacies of their life together she had found a freedom, but it was a freedom that sometimes filled her with a fear of those intimacies, a fear that such intense intimacies could only lead to pain, to an inevitable sense of horrible loss. And now that he was gone, she said she understood that he was gone, far beyond the pains and joys of their life together, beyond their intimacies and that fear. He was gone into another kind of freedom where, in her own death, she would never find him. Together in dying, but never in death.

Eyes Wide Open

I tell Jack, "I promised myself, this time I won't be in denial, not like I was with my father." Because my father had kept his fears to himself and was lucid to the end, refusing opiates, refusing religion and last rites, he'd had me fooled. I'd been sure he was coming home from the hospital after he fell down. He did not come home. This time, with Mom and Jack, I have my eyes open.

"My daughter," Jack says, "she's had my Jewish name changed so the angel of death can't find me. I told her she's wasting her money. Death can't find me. I'm never home."

He laughs. His mischievous grin, lips pulled back from his teeth, his dimples almost boyish.

Jack is watching me grieve. I'm watching him watch. Both of us trying to anticipate, to prepare. Jack says he smells fear on those who are going to survive him. He hates fear. He hates us watching him.

Jack's secretary tells me that he asked to know if her father had died a painful death from his cancer. She'd lied and told him she couldn't remember.

I overheard him in conversation on the phone, "This I can do. If it stays like this, this I can manage."

Jack doesn't ask me what my father's death was like, his actual dying. He knows I won't lie.

Strategic Planning

Bernie asks me how I'm doing. We're in his boardroom, and I'm bent over between his wheelchair and Jack's briefcase on the long walnut conference table. I'm putting Jack's briefcase back together at the end of our strategic meeting. We want to make our exit. There are 10 men around the table – all Bernie's financial advisors, accountants, comptrollers, tax specialists.

"I'm doing all right, Bernie," I say. "This I can handle – except for the torture hours between 2 and 5 in the morning. Thanks for asking."

Jack, impatient, is shuffling papers. He doesn't want Bernie asking me questions, doesn't want to hear my answers. He's pretending not to listen. If this were a courtroom, Jack would say, "Don't answer that question."

"I'm sorry to hear," Bernie says. A string of snot is falling unbroken toward Bernie's hands, hands that have been folded for him onto his lap. Bernie doesn't notice the snot.

"Thank you for asking," I say again, as I snap closed Jack's briefcase.

My senior partner says nothing, then calls for the male caregiver to wipe our client's nose. The caregiver is not there. He always slips out of the room during our meetings; he's always gone when our client needs him. Our meetings are the caregiver's respite.

Jack is not about to wipe Bernie's nose. Not that Bernie would let him. As he's said, he has his caregivers for that. Over his 20 years of increasing paralysis, Bernie hadn't expected any kind of caregiving from his wife. She had, however, increasingly cast herself in the role of the all-suffering wife for purposes, of course, of compensatory support, always trying to make her case for more money.

At some point, Bernie will lose the ability to swallow. But for now, his mind is sharp as a scythe, his eyes are still expressive, engaged. Eventually those eyes alone will talk, wanting only revenge and to cut a swath of escape from his body.

I contemplate gravity. What is it like to die slowly from the feet upwards?

Blood and Servants

"I'm only at peace with my blood."

Mom meant she didn't want a hired caregiver – certainly not the community care kind, not a Home Instead worker. That's who I was trying to hire so I could go to work, so I could "be a daughter, not a nurse. I'm not trained to be a nurse."

She kept firing any and all caregivers. That, of course, made her feel bad, so she gave each a set of pots, or her lavender soaps, as she sent them on their way.

"Your father worked a whole night in the sign shop to make a hundred dollars. I'll be goddamned if I'm going to pay some island lady 25 bucks an hour just to watch me sleep."

"I'm only at peace with my blood."

When it was the blood that was now killing her.

More Shtetel Wisdom:

"Man plans, God laughs."

Three Grains of Rice,
Two Pigeon Peas, and Jerk Chicken

Mom figured out real quick the ingredients of most dishes she tasted. She had a discriminating palate and could be as artistic with herbs and spices as Dad was with his colours. Nothing escaped her. So too Dad; he painted exactly what he saw – so laundry, wet clothes hanging on a line, are seen through a cathedral window in one of his Assisi paintings – exactly as he'd seen wet wash on a line.

In the weeks before Mom died, at her request and with Rose's agreement, I moved Mom from her Martin Grove condo to the Mountain Vista Village. I had stayed in Mom's room overnight. But I needed to go down to my law office to sign cheques and put out office fires before heading home to snatch a few hours of sleep. Rose came by to relieve me. I was glad for Rose's sudden company. Mom, too, enjoyed our being together. It became almost a celebration, since Mom was feeling peaceful after a brutal night. The morphine drip had beeped its warning until I finally got hold of a St. Elizabeth's nurse at 3 a.m. The nurse had had to come to the Mountain Vista Village all the way from Brampton to replace Mom's morphine cartridge. I was determined to keep Mom in the home in her bed-sitting room surrounded by the comfort of a few things, especially some of Dad's paintings.

"You think that this move here to Mountain Vista Village is going to give her joy? A couple of weeks of *joy*?" Elizabeth's voice had landed on *joy* like dog shit on a silver platter.

"Will I have to share this room with a stranger?" Mom asked me.

"No. This is your own room, to the end. No one will take this room away from you. You don't have to move, ever again. I promise you."

Neither food nor liquid had passed her lips in many days. Mom wanted to hasten death, but she also wanted to taste food, even though food made her sick. More than anything she feared asphyxiation on her own wretch.

Around 1 p.m., a healthy hunger overtook Rose and me. It was cold as I walked to a jerk chicken takeout place. I took heart at the normal conversation of working women coming off their night shift. For my lunch order, they recommended fish cakes, the jerk chicken, rice and pigeon peas.

Back at Mountain Vista Village, Rose and I sat in the window alcove of Mom's room, not wanting to disturb her rest. "This is so delicious. Who would have thought, a take-out place?"

"Can I taste?" Mom asked. We were incredulous. "But I don't want a lot."

We gave her three grains of rice. Two pigeon peas. A shaving of jerk chicken, counted out on a table-spoon.

She took this into her mouth, rolled it about her think-ing pallet, engaged, identifying. She beckoned for a Kleenex and I took the food out of her mouth. She vom-ited, a wave of dry heaves.

It was her last supper.

This Cup

> *My Father, if it be possible,*
> *Let this chalice pass from me.*
> *Nevertheless, not as I will but as*
> *Thou wilt…*
>
> —MATTHEW 26:39

> *Father, if this chalice may not*
> *Pass away, but I must drink it,*
> *Thy will be done…*
>
> —MATTHEW 26:42

And he prayed the third time,
Saying the selfsame words.

—MATTHEW 26:44

Why do I want to say the Bernie case is my Gethsemane?

Jack brought me into this file. Embattled, embarrassed, I've squirmed suffering all the way to the bank. I feel swamped by 33 years of Bernie's complex corporate history, tax-driven transactions, estate freezes. Jack and his *little-old-Jill-me* – going up the hill against seven strongmen and their foot soldiers.

Every time a door opened at settlement meetings, I saw several earnest juniors hard at work on their Apple computers, preparing for a paperless trial. Jack, well, he needed hard copies of everything. He was up to 67 Bankers Boxes, and still the case was growing.

But this has been more than the stuff of computers and boxes; it is years of a marriage come to nothing, love turned to hate, the in-sickness-and-in-health vow withering on the legal vine. Bernie's wife continues to torment him at every turn. If he asks that his meat be cut into small pieces, she cuts the meat into small slabs; if he wants big pieces of anything, anything at all, she chooses small. She leaves this ill man, her once-upon-a-time lover, helpless in his wheelchair. And so *he* shall leave *her* – *not one fucking cent*. Not one moment of gentleness (let alone regret) is left between them, after 33 years. Only hate. And money. More money. As much money. Any and all money.

Voicemail

I returned home to put out the garbage, threw in a load of laundry, checked the mailbox and the landline phone for messages, showered and changed. If I slept in my home, it was to snatch a couple of hours.

The voice messages were all from collection agencies hunting for my former husband, Zachary, those people on their headsets with their toneless voices, schooled in how to harass. Although we'd divorced more than 20 years ago, Zachary still gave out my good name in every one of his credit applications, if not at point of entry, then as soon as they soured. "This is an important message for Zackary Hamilton: *Do not ignore this message, get in touch right away, or risk an escalation of the matter.*"

I'd fought hard for this home – to save it for our son, Marco, for myself, to keep it out of the reach of venal creditors. Now, to go through this again – at this time of dying

– more than two decades after the divorce, yes, *as my mother lies dying, as Jack is dying.*

"Where did you get my number?" I demand to know, transferring my fury onto the representatives of Zachary's various credit companies. And in their tinny voices I hear that they are rattled by my attack.

"Mr. Hamilton must have given this number out as a point of contact, at time of borrowing, ma'am. It's not my fault."

Zachary denied it, of course. He has always been in denial.

"I know this woman," Jack had said to my then-husband, Zachary, when he had defended Zachary before the Law Society's discipline tribunal. He'd done so as a favour to me, his then junior lawyer. "She is an honest woman. She would never have done something as stupid as this." And turning to Zachary: "If you ever do this to her again, you will answer to me, personally."

The "this" was about the quick and duplicitous transfer of our matrimonial home into the nanny's name, then into mine. Necessary, because Zachary had been the solicitor for a group of investors, acting as the lawyer on their venture, and he was an investor himself. Knowing the market was going to tank, that the investment was in jeopardy, Zachary had conveyed away his interest, keeping this a secret from the other investors, who continued to pour money into the venture, borrowing funds on the basis of their personal guarantees.

"You must have gone crazy, to do something as stupid as this," Jack told Zachary. "I hear the music. *'Good idea at a bad time. I did it for my family.'* No, my friend, you did it for you. You have a serious problem." And to me, he had said privately, "This man will always be trouble for you. There will be no escape, unfortunately, now that you're connected through the child."

On the night I prepared several briefs in Zachary's defence, I worked into the wee hours of the morning, drinking Scotch, trying to explain why he had done it; why we had the title to the house transferred, trying it this way, then that, trying to make his actions credible: the transfer in consideration for the continuation of the marriage that at the time was in jeopardy; our disproportionate financial contributions to the running of the household, until I threw my pen into the air. "Why? *To defeat, hinder, delay and defraud your creditors.*" I laughed into the dawn, shameless co-conspirator that I was, a partner in Zachary's crime. Choking on the words. Choking on the Scotch. Choking.

"He didn't write this," Jack said to me, when he read the briefs that had been presented to the Law Society. "I thought not. Your husband is incapable of such brilliant advocacy."

Zachary got *only a two-month* suspension.

Within three months of that hearing, Zachary petitioned himself into bankruptcy, and walked away from his debts, his debris. Fifteen years later, Zachary's licence was irrevocably revoked, for some other dishonesty.

Apart from my father, Jack was the only man who had ever taken care of my interests. I owed Jack my financial life, and to a large extent, my emotional stability. When you owe, the debt needs to be repaid. You're indentured until it is. I carry that around with me. It is what has driven me. It is what has kept me back. That deep sense of obligation, to myself, to those I love. Sometimes, it has burdened me with shame, as when I fail, and I often fail, as in the case of Zachary. The man I married. My personal failure. My choice. So, while Zachary could have started all over again, it was me who could never be free. Especially not of my obligation to Jack. Never free. So I thought.

Graveyard Humour

There were two moments of unexpected laughter. I had forgotten to place a paintbrush in my father's casket. Knowing how distressed I was, my son, Marco, suggested I bury a paintbrush in the earth over his grave. The only soil I could move with my bare hands was at the foot of the stone. I pulled back the sod, and buried one of Dad's paintbrushes. Later in the spring, at Holy Week, Rose dug up the sod to plant perennials. She uncovered the brush. She never thought to tell me. A week later, she came back with a bouquet of brushes, planted these upright, so whoever had planted the original brush might wonder at its miraculous propagation.

The second laugh came at Easter when Rose, as she tended Dad's grave and that of her late husband, noticed another Melatti stone close by our father's plot. She was amazed to see that it belonged to our very alive older sister, Elizabeth Melatti-McFee, and her husband, Louie McFee. Elizabeth's name and Louie's were carved into a stone that lacked only their death dates.

Rose, going to the nearest dollar store, bought a wind-propelled Road Runner and some plastic fuchsia roses. She put these on top of the stone. When we all visited the graveyard with Mom (fortunately Rose gave Mom a head's up), Elizabeth cried, "Someone left roses on my grave."

"That's nice," Mom said. "Don't you think it's a bit premature?"

"Who'll tend to my grave, when I'm gone?" Elizabeth said. "No one will ever do for me what I've done for you."

"When I die," Louie said, "I'm going out in the biggest, badass, honking coffin money can buy, booze for my friends, Led Zeppelin, and Frank Sinatra, singing "I Did It My Way."

Gargoyles

In my dream, a living gargoyle is perched in the darkened corner of a room.

My mother's back is to it. She is looking at me. There is love in her eyes. Over her shoulder I can see the gargoyle. I dream speak to my mother:

"Don't look at it. Don't look into its eyes."

She turns and looks. I know that those eyes will kill her. Those are the eyes of my older sister, Elizabeth.

I try to tell myself it is only a dream.

Marijuana

At the beginning of the year of her death, when my mother
could still climb stairs and spend time with me at my home,
Mom sat in front of the fireplace watching Netflix and I
made our meals, under her tutelage. Sometimes she peeled
garlic or asparagus. She said she would love to be a sous-
chef, that she enjoyed peeling and chopping. I love season-
ing and mixing and using every pot in the house. I lay out
the plates, I go into the garden so that I can fill vases with
lily-of-the-valley in the spring, and tiny crabapples in the
fall.

Mom couldn't sleep, couldn't evacuate her bowels, and was
in constant pain, every joint. No appetite. In psychological
distress. When I recount these symptoms to a dentist at a
dinner party, his recommendation – marijuana.

Elizabeth, operating out of her silos of seized authority and acting as gatekeeper to Mom's doctor, was hor-
rified. As was her doctor. So, I asked my son, with whom
I'd had battles over this very issue in his teen years,
what he thought. The result: cookies appeared with
instructions from an unnamed nurse based in Ottawa.
A quarter cookie. Three hours to take effect. Eight to wear
off.

I told Mom I wouldn't give her anything I wouldn't try with her. She was good for the game. Along with almond-stuffed fresh figs wrapped in bacon, I served us the cookies.

All I remember is our discussing whether it would be better to die fully conscious of what is happening, or to die from dementia, Alzheimer's? At one point, I couldn't seem to remember how to end a sentence. Mom wondered about my eagerness for red wine.

Marijuana! We began to laugh. My son came to dinner and found his Nanna and Momma giggling like school-girls. Amazed, he watched us gobble up dinner. Then, his Nanna retired to the washroom for another marijuana-induced event.

On the ride home, my son said he had some joint pain (playing too much squash) and I told him he should get himself into a Jacuzzi with salts, but not just any salts – from the Himalayas, and on and on, obsessively, I went on about Himalayan salts, until Mom said, from the back seat. "I think you got the bigger piece of the cookie."

At the door of mom's condo, as I kissed her goodbye, she said, "It's too bad it has to wear off."

Prostate

My mother had withered to nothing, a stricken sparrow lying on her back, claws on the ends of spindly arms, with no wings to fly. Whereas Jack had grown enormous, swollen, probably because of the steroids he was taking. His eyes had turned wolf-white. He stared at me, inquiring.

"Why is our opposing counsel on Bernie's case so willing to oblige us, so eager *not* to adjourn the trial? She doesn't know how to play poker, that woman. It makes me almost want to request an adjournment, except that's not the way to play the game – to want something, just because opposing counsel so desperately doesn't want it."

Laundry

Mom did not think I should waste my younger years learning how to do laundry. All the time I practised the piano, learned to be a lawyer, and married my husband; my mother did my laundry. Zachary figured out long before I did that this was her link to me, a guarantee that she would see me once a week. Every now and then Zachary would slip his "boys" in with my "ladies," and they'd come back from my mother, pressed and in a separate bag. He thought this hilarious. And it was. It was also belittling.

My mother's work.

There is a white summer sweater I gave my mother to wash toward the end of her final summer. It wasn't that I couldn't do it myself. My mother had taught me how to roll the gently washed sweater in a towel, twist the towel to squeeze out the water without disturbing the delicate sequins and pearl buttons, how to block the sweater out on the clothes horse, how to make everything smell sweet. I gave her this sweater so that she could do for me what only a mother can do for her daughter, a form of communion. As I wear the fresh sweater the summer after her death, she is alive in the folds, the smell of her sweet handiwork wrapped like a gift in tissue paper.

My Last Request of a Dying Man

I go to see my senior partner at his home. I had asked Jack for this meeting, alone, as I had something important to ask of him.

"I have been changed, Jack, by caring for my mother. I am under doctor's orders to take a brief holiday, and this time it really has to be a holiday. Time away from the office to take care of a failing mother isn't a holiday. I need to go to Jamaica. And I can't return from Jamaica worrying about fighting a support motion, pending the trial. So I can't litigate, anymore."

He seems genuinely pleased by my request, that I have trusted him, trusted that he will understand.

"Have no fear. I'll enlist another senior counsel to work the case with me. He'll fight the interim motion, if need be. I'm trying to negotiate an advance on equalization that will obviate the motion. Go away. Have your little holiday. There's no need for anxiety. Anyway, you shouldn't be so emotional, not at your age. It's unseemly. You always took the practice of law too seriously. I'm only asking that you stay on the Bernie case until I die. After I die, you can do what the fuck you want."

We both laugh. Dying, he has found something he can give. Permission.

"Can I bring you back anything, from Jamaica?"

"Yes, rum. I make a delicious rum cake."

Home

"I didn't plan on losing my husband and my home in the same year. This is my house and I shouldn't be leaving it."

Mom had been shaking like a leaf. She wanted to visit her Veneto Drive home before the closing. She was already in her Martin Grove condo. Mom asked Rose to bring her back to her last marital home.

But Elizabeth was there, holding a mop, hands in pink rubber gloves. Elizabeth had the stairs cordoned off like the house was a movie theatre. Elizabeth would not let Mom climb the stairs.

Mom stood at the base, looking up past Elizabeth, and cried.

"This is my home. I should not be forced to leave. I have every right to be here."

In the kitchen, Elizabeth's anger sucked the oxygen from the room. She was furious. I had dared to open a cupboard – cupboards she had cleared. "I've done it all – *all*."

"You can take whatever you want," brother-in-law Louie said to me in the garage where he was cleaning up before the closing.

"Oh, I can, can I? Did my mother give you authority to grant permission?"

Passing out of the garage, I saw at curbside the yellow high chair in which Mom had fed her three babies, which our father had painted for her, which they had later used for plants at their last home together. The yellow high chair was piled high with other discards, left for strangers to take.

I should have claimed the yellow high chair.

Home

Lappin Avenue
Artavia Avenue
Dufferin Road, above the sign shop
The Haliburton Cottage
Veneto Drive
Martin Grove
Mountain Vista Village

Last night, a dream – the second of its kind. It was spring-time, and Dad was whirring along in a wheelchair. I was on my blue bicycle and Mom on foot, trying to keep up with him, as he went to post a letter, outside Veneto Drive. He seemed to be enjoying his motorized toy, had one foot folded up on the seat with an impossible flexibility. He was going to post a letter, something to do with his painting, and he was excited. We couldn't keep up. "Be careful," Mom was trying to urge him, as he ploughed through snow and then bounded up over banks piled high at the curb, seemingly invincible, certainly beyond risk. "I always knew he'd come home," I was saying to Mom, vindicated by this display. "No one believed it, but me. Look at him go." I was so very proud of him in my dream, as I was in life, proud of his determination, his will, his belief that he could accomplish anything – except his final wish – to come home.

Mountain Vista Village: In Mom's Room

Elizabeth sits in the room's window seat at Mountain Vista Village, reading the company's Client Care daily journal. The night personal service worker has made an entry in the journal, just before dawn:

"She wants to go home. She asked me the name of the home, the home before this one."

"I thought so," Elizabeth proclaims, as Mom sits propped by pillows, dying. My older sister is having a eureka moment, her vindication moment: now she knows for sure that what she's always believed is true – Mom hated moving to this room, her last home.

Elizabeth and Louie sit exactly where Mom wants no one to be, right in front of her. They sit examining her, watching her face, her closed eyes. Mom had asked me to pull her back from the window alcove because the light hurt even her closed eyes, she'd wanted to be pulled back into the darkness. And then she'd asked that I sit behind her – done this when she could still speak. She did not want onlookers. Even *in extremis*, she wished for privacy, she felt shame.

I am sure she hears Elizabeth making her point. But whatever the point is, our mother has lost all curiosity.

Later, past midnight, Mom's dying, I read the journal, waiting for the undertakers to arrive. I read how, even now, Elizabeth cannot resist proclaiming herself *right*. "I thought so, I knew so…*the home before this one was the right one.*"

It Breaks My Heart

.

Mom's litany:

"I never thought it would end this way."

"It came on, so suddenly."

"That I will never see my grandson marry."

"That I will never hold a great-grandchild."

"That I wasn't with your father, the night he died. I rushed home to cook a meal for your older sister and her husband."

"That he never said, 'Stay with me, tonight.'"

"That I somehow missed the signals."

"That I will never get to see your beautiful garden again."

"That I never let your father take a bath with me."

"That I never lay beside him on the hospital bed, worried about what the nurses might think, if they found us on the bed together."

"That you did not take the yellow high chair."

My litany of regret:

That none of us were there for him on his final night.

That Elizabeth hadn't phoned me and told me what he'd said, "Is anyone else coming, tonight?"

That not being there at the last, cancelled every day of the five months before.

That I had gone to a movie with my son, thinking *he needs me, too.*

That this was the last year I had my son at home, the year before he went out on his own, the year before my son became a man.

That I did not take the yellow high chair.

For This I Am Grateful

That you, my mother, got to my son's graduation, that you, my mother, saw him well up with emotion when they placed the ceremonial hood over his head and around his shoulders at the commencement ceremony.

That you, my mother, met the one he will marry, and saw them move into their first home together.

That you, my mother, got your will in the end, that your wishes were followed exactly for what should happen, after you were gone.

For this message you left, saved in my phone's voicemail:

It's 11 in the morning, and I know you're at work. I just wanted to phone you and thank you for such a lovely day, yesterday. You are so kind, and I love you – not because you give me things, but because I love you, from when you were a baby.

That you trusted me with your fear.

That I got to be with you in the end.

That you gave me life.

That you are my mother.

For laundry.

And she:

I am grateful that I got to spend 67 years with your father.

That I had a good life.

For the days you and I spent together, for those long drives.

For your company and conversation.

That you stayed nearby.

That you gave me the white sweater to launder.

That you came back for it, for me, when you said you would.

That I had *you* as my daughter.

Dreams

I dreamt last night that my mother was talking to her sister Sofia and I picked up the extension phone and overheard their conversation, my mother's sister, Sofia, being still alive, and it was Shrove Tuesday, but I didn't realize it until when I was walking toward my office and I saw people driving from early morning Mass, their rosary beads dangling from mirrors, a smudge of ash on their foreheads, and remembered that I had forgotten to meet my friend in the faith, a former Franciscan seminarian before he became a lawyer, and that I had missed our annual imposition of ashes.

And further on in the dream phone call, I eaves-dropped on Mom confessing her utter loneliness to her older sister, confessing that she felt utterly abandoned by all her children:

"Not by me, surely? Surely not me?"

"Why can't you love each other?" Mom asks. "You are sisters. Sisters!"

As for Elizabeth:

I have a dream in which she kisses me, mouth to mouth, and sucks my tongue out of my mouth.

Is this hatred? Fear? Self-aggrandizement? Self-pity?

I have no use for, or interest in, pity.

Sorrow, yes. Consolation, yes.

In a very real way, I love Jack, I even love Bernie, and I certainly love my mother.

But Elizabeth? Why can't I love her? Not even for the sake of my dying mother?

I have another dream:

"You know, you're dying, too," Jack says to me.

Then, not a dream, because Mom really asked me this, when I told her how exhausted I was:

"Do you have what is killing me?"

I dream everyone dies. The client Bernie Spurling. Bernie's soon-to-be-former wife, my senior partner, Jack, me. Death seems to be the only way to escape the burden of the case, the 33 years of Bernie's marriage. I am filled with panic. I've been given to panic all my life. In our early years, Jack had taken me aside and made me count to 10, made me breathe in deeply. "Now take that formidable brain of yours and apply it to this case," he had said, back when I was young and full of antici-pation.

"What I love about you is your passion for my case," Bernie says to me, in front of Jack.

You've got to be effing kidding, I think.

Jack pulls a face. "You don't have to be passionate about something to be an effective professional," he tells me. "You just have to stay grounded. It only takes one lawyer with brilliance to conclude a file."

My passion! I don't have passion. I have tenacity. I am a fraud.

Jack knows this.

I hate Bernie. Never more than when he displays vindictive avarice or says he loves anything about me. And I hate how he selects people to employ – defective people no one else will hire (like his comptroller who has a stutter and a limp), knowing that their handicaps keep them bound to him, that they work themselves to the bone for him, and knowing that they actually seem to give a shit about what happens to him, like I, too, being honest, actually care about Bernie, especially when he asks me about my dying mother. Yet I hate him. He has me flailing about in tortured confusion.

And it bothers Jack that Bernie seems to have affection for me. It is odd that Jack should be so possessive when it comes to this one client. He has never been so with any of our others.

I am here on this case – passion or not – to serve. Without question. Pretending never to be confused. Jack hates it when I ask questions.

I have regressed 30 years. I am again filled with self-doubt, like a junior lawyer. Working on this case has damaged me. I know with every face that Jack pulls, I have suffered another fall from grace.

"If you can't think, now, what will you do, when I'm dead?" I think he likes the shock value of the word. DEAD. Maybe saying DEAD somehow objectifies the

imminent reality. Dying. Death. Dead. Dead as a doornail.
DONE LIKE DINNER. DEAD RIGHT. DEAD
WRONG. DEAD END. DEADLINE. DEAD AS A
DOOR NAIL. WHAT IS A DOOR NAIL?

"What will you do, when I'm dead?"

"I will have frequent consultations with you, Jack.
You'll get no rest where you're going. I'll keep asking myself, what would Jack do, in this situation? And so I will
ask. I will hound you, even into death."

"I think you're going a little crazy. You will never be
able to think like Jack."

We both laugh.

Don't know that I want to. There will only be one
Jack. Never be another Jack. Never, ever again, in this lifetime, in any time.

Is it possible that I actually love Jack?

I hope not.

White Eyes

Jack has summoned me to his office. He has requested this
document, or that. We are preparing for questioning
Bernie's wife. I have brought Jack what he wants, and he
makes another request, and then another, and I am about

to rush off to fetch what he wants when he tells me, "Not so fast," and asks me to sit down.

He is eating a pear. The juicy flesh of it fills his mouth. He eats inward, tasting every bit of it, the juice running down his chin, which he ignores, as if he has lost feeling, or doesn't care anymore.

I smile and am about to giggle, like some silly schoolgirl, when he says, "What?" He is smiling, too, and we are both children again. I blurt out: "I'm busting to take a pee, if you must know, but you take first priority, Jack, as always." And he instructs me, "No, go, I don't want you to be in pain, I can wait" – which is a first.

"I'll be quick," and when I come back we are both giddy with the reality that it is finally happening, these cross-examinations of Bernie and his wife marching toward the trial.

He is asking questions out loud.

"Do you want me to take notes?"

"No," he says, and I sit there feeling useless.

Then I realize that I am a necessary audience.

He tells me:

"The cancer has metastasized. It is now throughout my liver, and beyond."

I wince.

"I will not live long enough to benefit from the cancer cures that will likely be uncovered within the next five years. I am happy. Death's natural. It holds no terrors for me."

He tells me what he needs me to do.

The junior and articling students are all running this way and that, and then he tells me he feels he must resign from the file.

"I do what I have to do."

There is one last story he says he needs to tell me. It is about his mother's secret. He says he had actually written the story down as if it were fiction. He has called the story "Miriam's Secret." He says the cleaning lady or someone in the house has thrown it out. The story is:

His father, David, had deserted his mother, Miriam, in the first year of their marriage. His mother's sisters had asked: *Was the problem, there* – signifying the bedroom? Her husband's abandonment must have devastated Jack's mother. In those days, no one divorced. *David didn't like the grocery business,* his mother told her sisters. They were dumbfounded. Each of them had a grocery store. It supported their families. They did not have a boss. How could someone not want to work in a grocery store? Getting Miriam's husband established in the grocery business had been the family's wedding gift. Her sisters, drained of their anger, took pity on Miriam and hugged her. *Poor baby. Don't worry, he'll come back.*

"Ten months later, when my mother returned home from work, she walked upstairs into the kitchen and there was my father sitting at the table, looking proud of himself. He looked at my mother, smiled and told her, '*I've found a job. I have a trade.*' I was born, nine months later."

Jack asked me if I could find a place, once he'd written it down again, to publish the story. That's what he wanted. The story was the truth. It was fiction but it was the truth. I was astonished. Because it *was* fiction, Jack knew that the story was somehow bigger. This from a man who hated untruth tellers.

"When this examination of Bernie's wife is over," I said, "say the word, and I will be there, morning or night. I will be your scribe, to help you get any of your stories down."

"There are so many."

He doesn't say *too* many.

I realize I may, in fact, have given him something. I may have given him a glimpse of life beyond death. His story, told.

This is short-lived. Within moments of my leaving his office, he calls me back.

He looks directly at me. I cannot read his expression. It is a poker face. I notice his white eyes. Not the living white-wolf eyes of a few weeks back. Jack's eyes were normally blue, but this is an almost metallic white. Is it the drugs? Is it some mineral, chemical compound that is burning them white?

He hands me the index to some brief we will need for tomorrow; he needs to have it sent out for overnight copying. There is a long silence.

He is not without fear.

(My mother's eyes were white, in the last week, a shocking contrast to the walnut of her life.)

"I am looking forward to tomorrow," I say, meaning that I am looking forward to his last cross-examination of a greedy wife.

He doesn't answer. He says nothing. Tomorrow has taken on a whole new meaning – tomorrow is something that may never exist.

Open Eyes

"You are likely sleeping with your left eye open," the ophthalmologist told me, when I complained of pain in my left eye, a pain that has frequently wakened me during the night.

"The pressure in both eyes is normal," the ophthalmologist assures me.

"How is that possible to sleep with your eyes open?"

"Babies do it all the time. Have you never watched a baby sleep, and you see the whites, just below the eye lashes? The eyes roll backward during sleep."

She gives me drops to alleviate the discomfort.

"You'll never know, of course, unless someone is watching you sleeping."

I hear: Don't shoot till you see the whites of their eyes.

I am safe. I sleep alone.

Questioning

Bernie: "We structured the transaction this way, in the event of my untimely death."

Opposing Counsel: "Or timely death…"

Jack: "Is death ever timely?"

Code of Conduct:
How to Behave Around the Dying

Do not burst into tears: The dying person should not be expected to console *you*.

Do not have your secretary cancel lunch, because you've been called to an emergency. There is no emergency greater than someone you love dying.

Do not refer to this person in the past tense in his/her presence.

Do not preach to siblings about the reality of a parent's imminent death: denial is protective.

Carry on life as normal, including telling the soon-to-be-deceased when he/she is behaving badly. Words near the end will never be forgotten.

Answer the question "If you can't think now, what will you do when I'm dead?" with honesty and creativity.

Confront all direct questions directly.

You'll know when you've said the right/the wrong thing.

Don't assume it's the chemicals talking: Dying brings a new honesty.

Speak your love.

Perform acts of empathy.

Touch, feel, smell, taste, listen; try these from the dying person's perspective.

Savour the juice of a pear.

Whatever you've determined to do differently, do it now; postpone no more.

Tuesday, March 3, 2015
Instructions for When I Die

When I die there will be no funeral,
visitation or reception.
I want to be cremated and I
want my ashes to be buried

with my husband, Giovanni,
at Prospect Cemetery
Section 38 lot 649, Cert#
MD99393.

At the burial I only want my
three daughters, my grandchildren,
and Louie
to attend the internment.
I want the Funeral Home to arrange
to have a priest say a Blessing at the
grave site.
There will be no Mass.
I also want my middle daughter to
say a few words about me at the
burial. (Make it brief.)
Only after the burial has taken
place, I want the death notice to
be published in the Toronto Star
newspaper.

I want these instructions carried
out with no changes or additions.

March 3, 2015

I left the office as quickly as I could, picking up veal cutlets for Mom and me, on the eve of my 63rd birthday. Mom was having another transfusion on the following day. Elizabeth "assigned" this transfusion to me. I told her I would be honoured to take care of Mom, on the eve of my birthday. What could be more fitting? The gift of blood on the anniversary of the day Mom gave her body and blood for me?

I know all this chaffed Elizabeth. *All* was her word. She forcefully resented that she always had to do it *all*. She felt that her sisters had always taken advantage of her goodwill and her husband Louie's, too, especially since he'd gone into retirement. She told me and Rose over and over again that they hadn't planned to spend their retirement as constant caregivers, responsible for every last little thing. *All* of it. Always.

"How convenient that you always have to be in Court? And what an inconvenience, that you ever had to be born."

The transfusions Mom and I managed to get done became a form of celebration. I took pride in getting her down to her blood test first thing in the morning, then back home and comfortable, and if the procedure had to extend into two days, I'd take her out for lunch or dinner, frail as she was. My favourite image is of Mom in a pink beret, purchased at the hospital gift shop, eating a Häagen-Dazs ice cream cone. I took my computer to the hospital to let her watch movies – *Roman Holiday*, with Audrey Hepburn, *Breakfast at Tiffany's*.

On the eve of my birthday, Mom talked about birthing her first child, Elizabeth. She talked about how afraid she had been, how overcrowded the hospital. They had placed her near the furnace room, in the basement. All that dark night she could hear the hospital furnace chuffing and feared that it would explode. Dad had not been allowed to stay with her, and the nurses were few in coming. It had been a very long and slow labour, Elizabeth eventually delivered with forceps, a bruising above her eye. When Elizabeth was three, Dad had to hold her down while the doctor squeezed the boil that had developed from her forceps birth. Those were the days when doctors operated on children without anesthetic, believing that tears dried quickly and that pain was forgotten.

There is a photograph of me taken while I was in labour. I am sitting in bed, my belly is round, taut, my eyes are closed, my hair is a wild halo about my head. It was a moment when I was in deep intimate communion with my pain. Years later, I thought to take a snapshot of my father in his last bed. His belly was distended from dialysis, his eyes were closed, his white hair was like an overblown dandelion. He was pregnant with death. I let him be.

I believe birthing gives a woman a preview of the final agony, what it will be like. Birthing somehow prepares a woman for dying. Of course, at the end of those birth pains there is a child. What lies at the end of dying?

Dare I call it a false pregnancy? What would that imply, what would that mean? That maybe we wait in queue for rebirthing?

On the eve of my birthday, Mom wanted to talk. For her, conversation had become a form of prayer. We talked late into the night. She gave me the story of my sister Elizabeth's birth and a message to deliver:

"Tell your sisters I loved *all* my daughters. I want you to emphasize the word *all*. I know all your strengths and all of your weaknesses, and I love you all, just the same."

Entrance Antiphon (Ash Wednesday)

Lord, you are merciful to all,
and hate nothing you have created.
　　　　　　　　　—WISDOM 11:24

Sins

My *original sin* vis-à-vis Elizabeth was the fact I was born. My *cardinal sin* was that I had a child, Marco.

My conception of Marco occurred at a time when Elizabeth's hormone therapies, everything she and her lawful Louie tried, failed. Month after month, Elizabeth's womb had continued to flush itself, until expectation dried and possibility vanished, irrevocably.

Elizabeth began to punctuate every conversation with the words "my infertility." Like the tolling of a church bell, Elizabeth intoned these words with a lofty solemnity, a resonant suffering, as if "her infertility" were now the one thing that set her apart. It was *her* infertility, her *own*.

Then came my "surprise child" – Marco – the child I never expected to have, the child Elizabeth believed I did not *deserve* to have, having no time for a child, what with my lawyering.

This was without justice. Without rhyme or reason. *Elizabeth had lived a virtuous life.*

Elizabeth's suffering had to have been terrible. The size of the hate it would become.

There is a photograph of Elizabeth in the hospital room, holding Marco. Elizabeth in this photograph is *longing. Longing to feed my child, longing to give what only I could give, what Elizabeth was deprived of ever giving. This is my body. It will be given up for you...* And there is Marco, asleep in Elizabeth's arms, dribbling my milk from the corner of his mouth, sleeping peacefully – or exhaustedly, having given up the task of sucking on nothing. For at the time I had been too thin to lactate adequately. I had to supplement, at six weeks, with formula, because the child born to me was "failing to thrive."

In the photograph, Elizabeth has become fat.

Surrender

"I am not afraid of death," said Jack. "It's the not knowing when, the lack of control over timing. If someone could tell me I had a week, I'd be okay with that. I've had a good life, good friends, enjoyed my work. I haven't been perfect by a long shot, but I have no regrets. It's the not knowing when."

"You are nowhere near dying, Jack," I told him. "Do you know what the last emotion was for my mother?"

Jack is genuinely curious.

"Shame. Not being able to do anything, not a thing, for herself. Brush her teeth. Sit and shit alone. Scratch an itch... You're nowhere close, Jack."

He looked at me; not so much inscrutable as already removed.

"The way the doctor told me," Jack said, "I thought was cruel. I was sitting in my hospital gown and he came into the cubicle in his scrubs, with a mask over his face. He told me straight away the cancer was inoperable, stage three-and-a-half, that I had three to six months to live, and to make an appointment with the oncologist…"

"So what did you want him to do?'

"Lie. Tell me to see the oncologist, explore my options. Where's the harm, to lie a little, leave room for a little hope?" Then he laughed. "My oncologist loves me. I've defied all the odds. So he tells me. And I believe it's true. I've pushed some limits. But our No-Frills doctor who delivered the news, he was a butcher in scrubs, a butcher of the spirit."

Golden Retriever Therapy

"Oh, God."

Elizabeth and Louie are seated at the foot of Mom's bed. My son arrives with Danielle, his bride-to-be, and their dog, Isis, who bounds with slobbering excitement into the room, smelling everything, even Elizabeth, who recoils in horror at the dog's lolling tongue. Marco has a coffee cup in hand, so when the diminutive Danielle lifts the 80-pound golden retriever over the bedrails to Mom's eye level, we were all thinking *Oh, God*. Mom can't take the pain of any kind of pressure against her bones. Held in the young woman's spindly arms, its back paws scrabbling about for somewhere to land, Isis looks frightened, panic-stricken. (Something like Mom when she had tried to swim.) Tenuous, I think to myself, everything – including the open-hearted love of a dog – it's so tenuous.

We hadn't known, on that day, about the acute bone-marrow cancer. There we were, gathered around Mom, *after the move to Mountain Vista Village,* and it was only then that a C.C.A.C. worker showed me a form that said: "Query acute bone marrow cancer." Not Elizabeth, not our family doctor, who had refused my request for a "family conference." In these dying times, what were we dealing with – confusion and misinformation. Elizabeth had been the self-appointed gatekeeper. Elizabeth, who had taken Mom to all her doctor's appointments. Elizabeth, who insisted that she had told us about the cancer in an email, saying that we never responded. False. This to be justification, in Elizabeth's punitive universe. The fact is, Mom had refused to subject herself to bone marrow aspiration, so any diagnosis had to be "inconclusive." Mom had told the doctor never to speak of the bone marrow aspiration test, ever again. She'd said she was never going to take the test. Her decision was final. Those doctor's visits were my older sister's domain. *She was the one who owned the information. She was the one who withheld it.*

This is what I have learned about dying: in and around the cancer; complaining, throat-slitting and indignation:

The rhythms of confusion, like contractions toward delivery, like waves coming to shore and receding, giving the odd respite, pulling and pushing by degrees.

"I was so sick that day," my mother said, "the day your son and his lady love came with the dog. It's such a shame. I really wasn't up to their visit."

I didn't know how to respond. Was it possible that Mom had thought she might get better?

"I think that dog really loved me."

"Of course the dog loves you. What's not to love?"

The Dark

"Dad-dy, I have to go pee-pee."

Elizabeth's voice called out, in the dark. Three years ahead of me, she had to be at least five. Rose was not yet born. I wore pyjamas, with a back flap. I crawled over the rails of the crib, and backed up to Dad whenever I had to go pee during the night, so possibly, I was two years old, and a bit. I was deeply resentful of the flap. I wanted pyjama bottoms I could pull down without having to wait for Dad to find my buttons in the dark.

Her voice would continue to rise, transposition of a half note, "Daddy, I have to go pee-pee," and then descend a minor third on the second *dy* of *Daddy*, raise the minor third for the balance of the phrase, then descend the minor third on the second *pee* of *pee-pee*, transpose up a half note, and repeat, louder and louder. I, of course, figured this out later, when I'd begun to study music. But at two-and-a-half or three, I wondered, at around the third sing-song transposition, what was taking him so long to respond, enough to shout out angrily in staccato: "Daddy-she-has-to-go-pee-pee," and our Daddy would finally come to take Elizabeth down the short hallway to the bathroom, where he'd sit on the edge of the tub, and when she had done her pee-pee, take her back to bed.

Without fear of the dark, myself, I began to wonder if my older sister was onto something. How to get our father's close attention?

And fear. I began to learn fear.

I knew she would.

Just as I knew she would die that day. And I was joyous. That her agony, finally, would be over. That *it* would be accomplished. That I had stayed the course. That I would be there at her end. That she would be released from her terrible suffering.

As I headed back to Mountain Vista Village, in the dark of that late November morning, mindful of the fact I was a few minutes past my time, that the night care worker would have left Mom's room at 7 o'clock that morning, I knew my mother would wait for me.

I was thinking of the words from a Kung Fu movie, words I thought I finally understood:

I would rather to have loved one single human being, than to be free of my own death.

I rushed into the room. Mom's eyes watching me. I whispered into her ear that *I could not have loved if I were never born, born to suffer and to die. Thank you for giving me life,* because without life I could not have known *this.* She closed her eyes, and opened them again, nodding her head twice, as if to say, *I'm glad for you. Enough. Now let's get*

down to the business of what's happening, here, right now.
Then her eyes widened, in horror, and she whispered, "I can't swallow," and she began to heave, dry heaves. I tried to lift her up in the bed, but the stone weight of her permitted no movement. I couldn't crank the bed. I ran into the hallway and called out, "She's choking," and five care workers arrived, and they got her up so that she could try to wretch into a bowl and when she could speak again she told them, "I want to be washed."

For five hours, fully dressed, she sat in her chair, the pillows supporting her. As I've said, she wanted me not to sit in front of her, not to look upon her face while her eyes were closed. She had me wheel her from the window alcove, back into the darkness of the room, where I sat behind her. A Filipino woman in uniform came in and prayed out loud for her, prayed that God would take her sister, her sister *who has suffered long enough*.

Amen. Amen.

I was sitting in the shadows with Mom when Elizabeth and Louie arrived. They sat in front of her, where Mom wanted no one to be. Elizabeth took our mother's head and held it against her breast, cradling her. Elizabeth asked me to report on when our mother had last eaten and last drunk something. I told her that to my knowledge it had been more than a week ago.

"Why can't I die?" Mom asked, whispering, querulous.

"I don't know, Mom. I don't know. I wish I could tell you."

Hours and hours, and still she is breathing calmly. She can't die.

Lunchtime comes and goes. Elizabeth murmurs to her husband about getting something to eat. I suggest they not eat in the room; the smell of food will make Mom wretch. What I really fear is that they will take the food on Mom's tray (they keep bringing food that is never eaten) and try to force her to eat. I fear Elizabeth and her husband will soon be sickened by Mom's smell.

The smell pools in the palms of her hands, it lingers on everything she touches and on all who touch her, a smell like an unclean belly button, like the rotten stump of an umbilical cord. Is it morphine seeping through what is left of her skin? She hasn't moved in hours, not a finger, not a toe. She is dying very slowly, from the feet up, from the inside out.

"Don't you want me to relieve you?" Elizabeth asks. This was supposed to be my day off and *their* day with our

mother. I say I'm not leaving. I will take a break later. *Go.*
I know you want to eat. *I know you are hungry.* Elizabeth
can't put off eating. She blames this on her hypoglycaemia,
but the truth is, she is fat and has never been able to put
aside a meal.

"I promise I will call you if anything changes." *Though they
didn't call me. Though they took our mother home, away from
our father on his last night. Though they left our father alone
to die, in the early hours of the next morning, on the day that
was to have been my time with him and our mother.*

Elizabeth doesn't trust me. But they do love to eat and
leave to eat.

Trust! Somewhere, someone has said it is harder to negotiate with stupidity than to engage with malevolence. Is
Elizabeth stupid or malevolent? When it comes to her, am
I being blindsided by my own stupidity, my own unknow-
ingness?

Why, in fact, has our condition – sister to sister – that
is, the way we immediately recoil from each other – always
been caustic, totally lacking in any semblance of trust? Our
condition! How could we have allowed our hate for each
other become greater than our love for our mother? De-
structive, without reprieve, even as we cope with our dying
mother, cope with the need for consolation.

Mom is utterly alone with her own dying. I am there, utterly alone with my thoughts. There is nothing I can say or do to comfort her, to comfort myself.

Mom's sinking into death is constant, except she signals me to lie her down. It takes five nurses for this final laying out of her still living body. She does not even whimper this last time.

I go to my son's house, which is five minutes away, pick up Italian sandwiches on the road, and when I arrive, Marco has opened and poured two glasses of red wine. After one glass, I am giddy. I cannot explain the euphoria. But then, on instinct, I call the phone in Mom's room and Louie answers. He tells me mother's breathing has changed.

"Have you told Rose?"

"Would she want to be here?"

"Of course she would. Why would you even think otherwise?"

Mom is on the bed breathing raggedly and there is the oxygen-conveying butterfly in her nostrils, the one intended purely for comfort, not to prolong life. When I arrive, they still have not called Rose, who has to drive in from Georgetown.

Who will be here? our mother had asked Rose earlier that week.

We will all be here, Rose had promised our mother. *All of your daughters will be here.*

Rose arrives in under 20 minutes. It is 4:30 in the afternoon.

Rose whispers, "I thought you said her breathing had changed?"

"It must be the oxygen."

Our mother's left hand begins to crawl up the bed, a hand I had thought dead. It moves along her body toward her face. She hooks her baby finger around the tube and pulls it down from her nose. Elizabeth fusses it out of our mother's hand, trying to force the tube back. I reach over the bed and take hold of Elizabeth by the wrist.

"Mom gets what Mom wants."

Our mother wails. Elizabeth backs off. It will be another hour before the ragged breathing returns. I am willing death to happen. It is as if the anger of her resistance has reinvigorated her life. It will take our mother until midnight to die.

We fall silent. We wait together.

Last Taps

Two notes rising. *Doh, soh*. I wonder, at first, if it is mechanical – coming from something in our mother's room? I start to hum the sound I am hearing. Sitting on the other side of the bed, Elizabeth ruffles her feathers in irritation. Can our mother hear the ruffle of feathers, of the Griffin? Of the gargoyle? I hear only Mom's shallow pant, and *doh, soh, doh, soh*, over and over again. Two notes attempting to rise, to lift off, not knowing what next, where next. Knowing only that it will end. *Doh, soh. Doh, soh....*

Kleenex

Louie, who has been perched all this dying time in the corner of the room, looking down at his pencil working on crossword puzzles, creeps up behind we sisters and pulls tissue out of a box, placing one beside each of us on the bed where our mother lies dying. It's like a magic trick, three tissues out of nowhere, at the absolutely appropriate moment. Only I don't cry. I laugh. I gulp the laughter down, so that, if my mother sees or feels anything, it is only the trembling of my body. I lay my laughing face against her stomach. I laugh silently into the belly that bore me.

My hysterical convulsing can only be taken for sorrow.
That is what it is.

Dust

"Remember you came from dust, and to dust you shall return."
—The Imposition of Ashes, Ash Wednesday

The interiors of her homes were meticulous, cared for. The expression, "You can eat off her floors," was made for my mother. One of her projects for the apartment, where we lived above my father's sign shop, was to remove the yellowed wax from the linoleum floor of the rec room.

When my father expanded the sign shop to accommodate transport trucks that entered through a huge garage door, the expansion gave our family a recreation room, and Mom got a laundry. This freed her from having to take our laundry to a machine inside the sign shop, where customers would ogle her young figure in her house dress.

Because of her constant waxing and polishing, over the years, the linoleum of the rec room had yellowed. She decided to attack it. As I practised the piano, Mom was on her hands and knees. I vowed *never me, never me, never me on my knees.* Mom soaked the squares in solvent and then scraped each square with a paring knife until the linoleum regained its luster. She never asked her daughters to help. She thought we had better things to accomplish in our lives.

The floor looked awful, at first, being two-toned. But once she'd started, there was no going back. The complete cleaning took her about a year. On Sunday nights, our family sat on a long yellow vinyl couch, watching *Bonanza* and *The Ed Sullivan Show* in black and white, while she worked on the floor.

"Come watch," Dad would coax. "Aren't you even going to sit down?"

"I can hear it," Mom would answer, as she attacked the floor.

By Christmas, she'd worked through half the squares, edging backwards, crablike, crossing in front of *How the Grinch Stole Christmas*.

It seemed futile, one square at a time, and yet she got it done, achieving a dignity underfoot.

I inherited my Mom's discipline, her tenacity – a gift given in the blood. Elizabeth turned the same gift into bloody-mindedness, a sometimes mendacious manipulation of others. Rose grew up mastering the art of doggedness, a concern for concentrated clockwork routines, her family and cooking. And as for me, I went to work on the piano – becoming a young woman who played, I am sorry to say, like I was cleaning linoleum. Of course, I got my Associate Diploma from the Royal Conservatory of Toronto, and I played a solo piano recital, exercising the very same discipline that would carry me through law school, into a career that became my daily bread for over 30 years, a career I rarely loved. You work, and work, and work, and sometimes the work is excellently done, but then one day you feel spoken in your bones a word…

Dust.

"I'm going to puke," she whispered.

Though she weighed less than 90 pounds, I couldn't lift her. She lay pinned by her shoulder blades to the bed, head to the pillow, and I couldn't move her. I am strong but I couldn't move even one shoulder, couldn't roll her on her side into the "rescue" position. How could *almost*-dust be so heavy?

Ysatis

"What is that perfume?"

The young man outside the L.C.B.O. is trying to sell me a box of chocolates, raising money for some cause.

When I refuse, he offers to carry my box of bottles to my car. Again, I decline.

"Please, let me do my good deed for the day."

I look into his eyes. He's about age 13, a simple, open, honest kid – probably he's been bullied for his decency. So I let him carry my box to the car. When I offer him five dollars, he won't take it. He says the school authorities who gave him the chocolates to sell count the boxes and he can't end up with more money than the actual number of sold boxes. So, I take a box and allow him to give me change, and then he asks about my perfume.

"Ysatis by Givenchy," I tell him. "It was my mother's perfume."

"Reminds me of my Nanna. Smells just like her. I loved my Nanna. She just died. I really miss her."

"My mom, too. I miss her, too."

Dust has its smells. Sometimes linoleum. Sometimes Bankers Boxes. Sometimes perfume…

My Senior Partner's Last Instructions

Jack called me into his office to inform me that the new senior litigator, who was taking over my role in the Bernie file, wanted to build his own team. After three decades in the practice of law, I am enough of a businesswoman to know the financial implications for me. The loss of income. No matter. Once again, I'd learned something from Jack. I gave him permission.

"I am fine with it, Jack. I will support the new lawyer in every way he needs, transitionally. All will be well with the file and with Bernie."

Jack closed his eyes and opened them again, decision confirmed.

He was very thin, except for his belly, distended, which he rubbed with both hands, like a man content with his meal. Leaning back in his chair behind his desk, he was sweating, but it was not a summer sweat. The air-conditioned office was cold to the point of making me shiver. It was as if Jack were in labour…even talking had become arduous. There was a wild look in his eyes. I imagined a coyote scrabbling to escape a trap, gnawing on its own leg bone until futility at last took over, giving way to exhaustion.

"I am not afraid of death," Jack announced. "Death is natural. It holds no terrors."

"Death doesn't frighten me either," I say. "It is the *process* of dying I worry about."

"You don't have to fear that nowadays. Doctors will assist you to die, if you tell them you're ready to let go. We are hard-wired to want to live, until the suffering becomes unbearable."

"Why don't you fear death?"

More and more he'd become a teller of quick stories. He told me two.

"When I was four, my father said to me, 'Do you worry about waking up when you go to sleep? Death is like that; you just don't wake up.'"

Then Jack told me about a mortician he had acted for on some commercial litigation case. The mortician told him that, ironically, he abhorred being around dead bodies. His life's work had driven him to drink. "You're not afraid of death," Jack had said to the mortician, "you're afraid of living."

"My mother thought dying was the most important thing that had ever happened to her," I told Jack.

"Well, your mother was wrong. And I hope that wasn't the case. I hope more important things had happened to her in her life. Living is more important than dying. Dying is just one little part of it. Death doesn't change who you are or what you have accomplished. It's just a bump in the road. A big bump, but a bump nonetheless. Death will happen to you, too." He looked me in the eye. As if this were *NEWS*. As if I didn't know that I'm next.

"My palliative doctor is funny," Jack went on. "He won't talk to me about dying. He plays all around it, like a kid with a spoon pushing his peas around on the plate. Life is full of problems you have to solve, peas you have to swallow. Dying is just one of those peas."

Again, I remembered my labour pains, the 40 hours of it, tolerable until I gave up and let them perform the Caesarian section. At that point, they couldn't take the baby out of me fast enough. I wanted it over. Those minutes they took to prepare me for surgery, they were worse than the 40 hours.

Natural anything is overrated, whether it's birthing or dying.

I was euphoric as I left Jack's office. My senior partner! I felt like a kid being let out of school, for the summer holiday. Yet by the early hours of the morning, those hours between sleep and waking, I was in a panic again. Over so soon? After 31 years? The demands on me as a lawyer had burned away the hours like human hair being put to a lit candle. How do you *just stop*? Walk away? Or do you keep practicing until the practice stops you?

Passover

"The grain of wheat must die or it remains just a grain of wheat; but if it dies bears much fruit."
— John 12:24

On a day in mid-July, Jack admitted himself to Sunnybrook Hospital, into the palliative wing. Neither food nor drink had passed his lips for three days; He was seriously dehydrated. Our junior lawyer, Lydia del Broco, thought he was going to be *just fine*. "Jack is all about food, and as soon as he starts eating again, Jack will be just fine."

"No, he won't. Jack *will* die. Jack *is* dying."

I had been to the school of dying.

The Fall

I was just outside our law chambers. I'd hoisted my handbag and three heavy briefcases – one on wheels, two others slung over my shoulders – down the stairs to the sidewalk. I plunged face-first into the asphalt street, briefcases still in hand. A van braked close to my head. A young man in a Canada Post uniform got out, shaking.

"Is my tooth bleeding?"

"No, but your nose is."

He got me wet wipes and Kleenex from the van, and I retreated to the stairs of our building, and I just sat down there on the cement stairs as bloody bruises blossomed on my knees. My black jacket was ripped at the elbow.

I called for no one.

I spat out dirt in the underground garage and on the drive home.

I poured myself an Epsom salts bath and scrubbed away at my body, as my mother had done when, as a child of six, I had skinned my knees on cinders (some of those cinders are still imbedded under my skin and I'm almost 65).

Serves me right, I reasoned, that I should suffer such a humiliating fall in front of the law chambers where I had laboured so resolutely yet reluctantly for more than three decades.

Everything ached, body and soul.

On a Friday evening, *31 years ago*, one of Jack's clients, Tom Mackenzie, who was a very rich man, called the office at about 7 and I happened to answer.

"Did I leave my briefcase in your office? Could you go look for it?" And then, "What are you doing, still there? What are your plans for tonight?"

I was then what our current junior lawyer, Lydia Del Broco, is now – a brainy woman, "married to the job." At first, I didn't get it.

"I'll tell you who's attracted to you," Jack said, the next Monday. Tom Mackenzie owned his own insurance business.

"He's on his third divorce," I protested, and added, "there's this man, Zachary, I've been dating. He seems to like me."

"Hello," said Jack, shaking his head at me. "Wake up, woman. What's not to like about you? And don't dismiss the notion of Tom so quickly. It's as easy to fall in love with a rich man as a poor man."

I had felt nothing but contempt for women who landed on their backs under rich sacks of suet, knees in the air.

What I hadn't foreseen was how arduous marriage would be.

Shame?

I saw in the mirror my raccoon eyes, the split under my right nostril – aftermath of a fall that shouldn't have happened. Here, at the end of my career, loneliness rose up. And a terrible feeling of waste. For a moment, I felt overcome by a sense of devastation – the hours, and hours, and hours – to what end? This end. An unattended fall to my knees, on my face. Eating dirt.

Still! No bones broken. I had survived my husband's bankruptcy. I had raised a son, with only me as a bulwark between Marco and the darkness. I'd got him through university and he'd graduated without student debt. He now works in the Alberta oil industry. He's in love, has bought his first home (in Calgary: life can't be perfect), and soon he will be married.

I put on sunglasses before going out. Like one of those battered women whose cases I'd taken on over the years.

Shame? Yes and no. Maybe a little. But mostly nobody needed to see my raccoon eyes.

"Stupid," Jack had hollered at young me in the firm's reception area, in front of a client, Fiorino DiMarco, a developer. All because I had taken a few precautionary moments to photocopy a document critical to a case lest it disappear into the chaos of Jack's office.

After Fiorino DiMarco left, I went into Jack's office. I closed the door quietly. I spoke barely above a whisper, something I had learned from Jack.

"You will notice I have closed the door so that no will ever hear what I have to say to you. This is because I have too much respect for you, Jack, to do to you what you just did to me. You are trying to groom a firm of litigators. You are creating a firm of mice. I will never be able to work again with Fiorino DiMarco, before whom you have just called me 'stupid.' *I was covering your ass,* Jack. I took seconds, Jack, seconds, to photo-copy a document that I knew you would *lose*. I acted to your benefit, Jack. Like I found you the smoking gun in that case last year, from which you made a-quarter-of-a-million dollars. If you *ever* call me stupid again, I will quit, on the spot."

I walked out, slamming the door behind me.

Jack didn't come out of his office for hours.

He never called me stupid again.

And I never quit.

"Just stick with the Bernie case, until I'm dead. Then you can do what the fuck you want."

Before Jack died, before he could see the Bernie case through to its conclusion, I did have one final chance to say:

"Jack. We have to talk. It's like I've done no right."

"You've done plenty right. We don't have to talk. You don't have to take the practice so seriously. It's not like it's your life. It's not the whole of you."

What God Forgot

He told me a story by a Yiddish writer, about this guy who dies and when he passes on, God's Book of Judgment is opened and it turns out that his bad deeds are evenly poised against his good deeds. So, they don't know what to do with him. They give him a feather and send him back to Earth, so that his next choice of good or evil will tip the scales.

"I think the creator of that story got it wrong. There needs to be a third scale – for honest mistakes."

Resurrection

I called my son. I couldn't bear to go through the drawers and armoires full of Mom's clothing. I decided to give most of it to Naija (my son's former nanny) and Afi, her cousin. Let them decide what to keep, what to bag for Goodwill or Crippled Civilians, what give to her Jehovah's Witness colleagues.

Naija and Afi live in adjoining apartments on the first floor of a building on Old Weston Road. We brought in 10 garment bags and four green garbage bags full of clothing. I felt enormous relief. (Now I wouldn't have to face the burden of how to integrate Mom's clothes with mine, the distress of seeing her clothes on my own aging body.) Afi promised me, unsolicited, "I will call your names whenever we wear one of Francesca's precious clothes."

When next we spoke on the phone, I learned that among the bags was an elegant suit.

"The grey one, with the pinstripes, a long jacket, below the knees, about the same length as the skirt?"

"Yes, that one."

"I loved that one. My mother bought that at The Room. Today, it would sell for a couple of thousand dollars. Mother had classic taste. Nothing ever went out of style and she, of course, took such care of everything, not a thread out of place. I thought it would look stunning on Naija."

"She's allergic to wool, so we gave it to one of our sisters. She's a tall, elegant woman, straight in her back. She said only the waist needed to be taken in, so you can understand how shapely she is. It has found a good home."

Sometimes, I imagine answering the front door on a Saturday. The stranger will be a black woman. She will hold a tract in her hand, and carry a briefcase. She will be a Jehovah's Witness, and she will be wearing my mother's suit. I will reach out and embrace her, and smell my mother's perfume rise from her black skin. She will be my mother. I will be seeing her, once again.

Empty Fields

One sunny Sunday in late August, just before I started kindergarten, my father took me with him to a clothing factory outlet. He had to mount a sign for Eliot Atkinson in an adjacent open field. Dad dug postholes and I held the post, while Dad filled the holes. I remember the sound of wind, the rolling crunch of a single car passing on the dirt road. We were alone. I played in the empty field, chasing clicking grasshoppers through the tall dry weeds that scratched my bare legs. The cricket chirps were accompanied by the high sawing of the praying mantis; it was like the high sound in my middle ear that is the sound of my own blood circulating. From that field, I could hear my father's hammer, banging nails into the sign he had hand-painted back at his shop, United Signs and Outdoor Advertising. And then, I was back in that tunnel of my night terror, only this was day, and this horrible feeling began to close around me. It was a growing feeling that came up from my stomach and pushed the air out of the air, as if there were no forward or backward through it. *Why am I here?* In the blinding light of summer's day, I stood alone in that empty field, unable to move, paralyzed by the terrible fear. I didn't even hear my father calling me once his job was done. It was as if the insect sounds and every other noise had been sucked from the field and I was deaf and lost in a thick silence.

"What happened?" my father asked. I remember staring into his eyes, bewildered, staring at the question, before burying my face in his chest.

> *Why was all this shown to me*
> *If I would not be allowed to keep it?*
> —*POMEGRANATE MOMENTS*, GALE ZOË GARNETT

Cosmic Conversations

Father, why would you have given me all this, if only to take it all away?
    Silence.
    Can you hear me?
    Silence.

Am I all that I am supposed to be?
Silence.
Did I make enough of your gifts?
Silence.
Is there such a thing as an empty field?

Our mother died disappointed, believing she had failed as a mother. "Why can't you just love each other?"

Our father died disappointed in his daughters, feeling he had failed as a father.

"How did you all come from your sweet mother? From me? This thing where you keep going for each other's throats, it means you won't ever be there for each other, not to celebrate each other's joys, not to mourn each other's sorrows. How long can you live with your refusal to forgive?"

The First Art Lesson

Three sisters, aproned and seated on overturned Coca-Cola cases before easels and Masonite boards. We watch our father divide space on his own board with a piece of charcoal, making the wonderful scratchy yet sensual sound of charcoal against Masonite.

"You start by finding your horizon."

We stared at our boards. Blank, featureless. Rose began. Being the youngest, she had no inhibitions. I could see over her shoulder. She drew an uncertain, wobbly line. Dad said:

"The first time you take a crack at a painting, you try to cover the whole canvas so you have a feeling of where everything is, finding the darkest things. Snow isn't just white. Snow, when you really see it, can look like it has a bruise."

We tried to brush colour onto the Masonite. Rose moved a glob along the board, thinning it out. "Like this, see, make Xs," Dad guided. He'd been brushing-in the shores of a river in his landscape, X-ing in shadows, dimpling the flat spaces where there were hollows. We began to work in a second colour, Dad telling Elizabeth not to peck like a bird, telling us not to blend and blend until the values of each colour disappear in a flatness, telling us there'd be no contrast to anything if we did, there'd be only a sameness, no volume.

"Don't expect it to be there all at once."

While we painted, he spoke:

"Great art is made through contrast. Darkness brings out the light. Every colour has its own values that move from its darkest shade of itself toward its own light. When you paint for a long time, you begin to look at the world around you and read its shape through colour. Only after you see and paint the shape do you add texture – bark on a tree, waves across water. The texture of the world is its detail. Contrast is its essence."

By our third lesson, violet shadows began to appear in our snows, yellows and browns, and a cluster of trees in the distance, a mysterious smudge of violet, the icy sky the same colour as the river, except the water had a deep gash where it drove deeper. Rose's trees had become thick stumps, staining her snow like bulbous clumps of brown dung. Rose started to cry. She wanted her trees to be lean, elegant. I couldn't stop laughing, thinking her fat stumps were wonderful.

"Do you know it all, do you?" Dad asked Elizabeth, who sat, arms crossed, frowning, furious because Dad was deftly making her river water move on the board, brushing quickly until, exasperated, Elizabeth's voice went up in a howl of protest.

"It's not mine anymore."

"How do you expect to learn anything, if I can't touch it, can't show you?"

Dad threw down his rag and said he was fed up. We fell silent. And then went upstairs, to wash before dinner.

Dad stayed alone in his dark sign shop, cleaning and reshaping our swollen brushes.

Looking back, I can see that it is no good trying to teach your child what you know because what you learn in this life, you learn on your own. You learn how to live with yourself. You find out that you are what you seek, right there, in the beginning.

Amatavi

Our mother frequently told us the story of the death of her father, Rosario. I can still see what she saw, the bed in the basement of a little house on Lappin Avenue – *Nonno* Rosario surrounded by all those he had loved and who had loved him, Mom saying that Dad had seen a shadow pass the basement window just as Rosario raised his right arm three times from the elbow, in a kind of wave to include all who were around his bed. Before he let his hand fall back onto the covers, he said:

"*Amatavi.*"
"*Love each other.*"

My sister Elizabeth insisted on an apology for something *I had not said*. Not just any apology but an abject apology, and she said she would be the judge of its sincerity. The apology was to be for something I allegedly said to our sister Rose. I hadn't said it, and I couldn't lie and pretend that I had. But Elizabeth insisted that I'd said it, even though she wasn't even there to hear it, preferring Rose's reported truth to mine.

I went to my father for his counsel. He said: "Surely there is something for which you can be sorry, without having to eat your sister's shit?"

Forgive me, Elizabeth. For this, I am truly sorry:

For not listening to your pain. For letting your anger push me away. For letting it damage me, damage our little family, damage our father's and mother's last years, even unto their final hours. When even on their deathbeds, I could not prevent myself from feeling hate. I am sorry for not being able to extricate the "you" from "me," for allowing myself, even for those precious moments, to become … you.

And I am so very sorry they had to take their knowledge of us into their final breaths.

Amatavi. Love each other.

Yiddishe Kop

Jack's death *was* the negotiation of a lifetime, and he used his death as a bargaining chip – brilliant strategist that he was. There was no way Jack was going to let Revenue Canada outfox him, out-manoeuvre him, get at his estate.

He had his mysterious ways. When Revenue Canada wouldn't accept his unpaid-taxes proposal, Jack petitioned himself into bankruptcy.

He lived 18 months beyond his doctors' projections.

How *did* he do that, live 18 months, suffering with pancreatic and liver cancer?

Any conveyance within three months of personal bankruptcy is *presumed fraudulent*.

After six months, there's a *rebuttable presumption*.

Over a year. . . Jack made the ones he loved *home free*. *Everything out of my name, into theirs. Nothing left in my estate*.

Jack, who could will just about anything, willed himself to live beyond the fraudulent preference and rebuttable presumption periods. He caused the petition to be served upon admitting himself into palliative care at Sunnybrook – days before he died. Brilliant strategist? He certainly was. Jack was all that.

Forgiveness

Forgiveness, like faith or love, cannot be willed. I know intellectually that unless I forgive my sister and myself for the pain we inflicted on our mother with our quarrelling, I will never be free. I also do not recognize myself, a normally compassionate person, in the lack of compassion I feel for Elizabeth. If I permit myself a scintilla of softening toward her, I am afraid I might be sucked back into her vortex, for collateral, self-serving reasons having nothing to do with true forgiveness or love.

My rational self tells me to protect myself, as I tried to protect our mother. My soul self tells me that unless I love my sister as myself, I am damned.

Sometimes, I worry about what might happen if her husband dies before Elizabeth. What if she reaches out to me to help her – whether to be her driver to the hospital or just to get her out of the house? How could I refuse her? And then I remind myself how she told me the only reason she required me to visit the assisted-living facilities, nursing homes, all the alternatives for our mother, was that she doesn't drive. Otherwise, she'd have done it herself. She'd have done everything, herself. She hated to need me, in any respect.

Rose, she needed. Emotionally. Elizabeth could not comprehend Rose's rejection of her – Rose's push-back for all the unwanted help and intrusions in the aftermath of Rose's husband's death. That was the year before our father died, followed three years later by Mom's death. As Rose had tried to mourn Carl in her own way, on her own terms, Elizabeth and Louie just arrived unannounced, to take charge of it all.

"Today, we're going through Carl's clothes."

"No, we're not," Rose answered. "I'm packing up Carl's clothes when it suits me, not on your timetable." But Elizabeth didn't get that. Elizabeth saw her impositions as acts of charity – gifts, the rejection of which left her bewildered and angry. *How could Rose, after all I have done for her and the kids?*

Me, she had hated from birth. Nothing I could say or do would ever surprise Elizabeth in its capacity to betray her.

Compassion is an exercise, so I force myself to contemplate the uncomfortable. I force myself to remember the day that Elizabeth and her husband showed up at our mother's condominium, unexpectedly, when Rose and I were there together with Mom, happy in each other's company as we went about whatever we were doing – Rose dusting or sorting laundry, me working on those Bankers Boxes full of Bernie's financial disclosures.

Elizabeth and Louie didn't call up from the intercom in the lobby. (They never did. Our mother hated the way they would just arrive, unannounced, while she might be on the toilet, in the middle of a bowel movement, humiliated at their unexpected arrival without the courtesy, even, of a knock.) As usual, they used their fob to get into the building, and when we heard the key, scratching in the lock, Rose and I froze.

Our silence reminded me of the silence of little birds on my trip to Siena, my summer abroad before I started to practice law – dozens of caged birds kept in a garage for killing and then eating, as these little birds are considered a delicacy in Italy. The garage door was left a foot open, to permit for air and sunlight, and whenever I walked past, the birds would fall silent, as if anticipating the door to be lifted, the culling of the caged choristers that would then take place. They knew this, the birds, they knew what this meant, this passing of the human shadow. And yet every day, after a few moments, the raucous singing would resume, life would resume.

"Do you know what it is like," Elizabeth said, "to walk into a room and hear your own sisters fall silent?"

Elizabeth had wiped the table clean. Roughly, she seized each one of my Bankers Boxes and piled them against the wall nearest the door, and then put on the kettle for tea, opened the refrigerator door, and began a noisy decluttering, tossing full containers into the garbage, without concern for recycling the jars, or knowing if the contents were today's meal or yesterday's leftovers – throwing out everything except what she herself had made.

What could anyone say?

"I feel for my daughter," Mom had said. "She's my daughter and I love her. It hurts me to think of her dying, alone."

Some two years after our mother's death, I have a dream that we are all around Elizabeth's last bed, including our mother. She has the comfort of the pure oxygen at her nose, the identical clips Elizabeth had sought to reinsert into our mother's nostrils. In the dream, our mother pulls the tubes away from Elizabeth and says, shockingly, "I want her to feel what I felt. I want her to know what it felt like, even as I lay dying, to be forced against my will."

Mom would never have said such a thing. She was incapable of even thinking it, forgiving as she was, unto death.

"*I know she meant well. I know she really thought that what she was trying to do was all for the best.*"

I remember:

"What do you think this move to Mountain Vista Village is going to give her? A couple of weeks of *joy*?"

And if it had given even the possibility of joy, would there have been any harm in that? Was it not worth the try? What if the move to Mountain Vista Village was something *our mother had wanted for herself*? Why did it have to be Elizabeth's preferred choice? That's a choice she'll get to make for herself. Or maybe she won't. Maybe that's what the dream was all about, telling me more about the dreamer than the subject of the dream. Maybe I wanted Elizabeth, finally, to have some insight into what it was she had done.

So, I can't reach out to her. Knowing that she will never reciprocate. Knowing that she needs to cling to that sense of herself as always being right. And that will be her comfort in her hour of death. She will go down with two fingers in the air. Forgiveness withheld from us both, from the only ones who can truly give it to each other.

Denial

The voice-activated email from Bernie comes copied to Jack's entire litigation team. No one has thought to put up an out-of-office message, but that was never Jack's style, in any event. Jack prided himself on accessibility. And, in fact, there was one email from me to which Jack did respond, even after checking himself into palliative, to tell me that "I am so very, very sick. I am so very, very sorry."

So, Bernie writes:

"I don't understand about these undertakings. Jack? Why do they keep multiplying document requests like the *effing* sands of Arabia? Jack?"

Jack?

I think: The client doesn't know. Is it possible that Jack never told Bernie? About his death, upcoming? Never put it on the table?

Death

"He died... Their wailing was not only for the one who had died but for themselves, leaderless without him."
> —THE FIRST MUSLIM: THE STORY OF MUHAMMED,
> LESLEY HAZLETON

Shovelling

The rabbi explains that shovelling dirt onto the coffin is a traditional sign of respect, to ease the pain of loss, and that casting earth from the back of the shovel is a way of showing sorrow at the loss, a reluctance to let go. Further, the grave must be entirely filled before anyone can leave the site.

I shovel and I shovel, my high heels sinking into the soft earth, my black hat cockeyed on my head, but with the back of the shovel, I can't get much done. I can feel the restlessness of my male partners. This is not for me. I must renounce the shovel. Which I do reluctantly. Bernie, who has come as close as he can in the wheelchair, asks his personal caregiver to shovel for him.

"I'll tell you who should be in that grave." Bernie calls out, to the horror of Jack's mourners, the name of his wife of 33 years: NAOMI.

Jack Predicts

"Every case ends, eventually. A final judgment. A settlement... Bernie's case will settle. Bernie doesn't want his family put on display for public amusement. He'll stop the circus just short of a trial."

"Human beings." Jack laughed. "I'm going to miss all this. I won't make it to Bernie's divorce party. But you be sure to go. It's about time you had some fun."

The Dream

It is the night before Rosh Hashanah. I have this dream about Jack:

My sister Rose and I, after a day of pilgrimage, have checked into an inn for the night. We have been walking the Camino in northwest Spain and are hunkering down in a high-end hostel, which is not a youth hostel or communal bedding place with bunk beds, but is a government-converted palace. We have our second-floor room with twin poster beds. Rose has gone upstairs to settle in for the night. I am in the bar, ordering a Scotch.

Jack calls to me: "You're not drinking that cheap bar swill, are you?" He is sitting outside at a picnic table in full sun, his curly hair incendiary with sunlight. With that boyish smile of his, he motions me toward the tables.

I step out onto the patio and into a blinding sun.

"Taste the good stuff," and he points me to a bottle. It is detailed in gold filigree, like a Fabergé egg. He pours out an amount and indicates that I should not sully it with ice or water, but take it neat. "Neat means straight," Jack teaches.

And I do. I have never tasted anything like it – ambrosia.

At this point, I notice one of the lawyers from our chambers sitting quietly off to Jack's left. Jack pours our colleague a generous portion.

"Do you think you should be drinking, Jack, in your condition?"

Jack gives me that look to quell impertinence. We both laugh at my absurdity, trying to counsel Jack.

"Would you like some more?"

"No, Jack. I've got a long way to go, tomorrow."

Inside the inn, I turn and look back. Jack waves from the picnic table, raises his glass in salute.

I wake suddenly in my own bed in Toronto, feeling euphoria, a sense of well-being permeating my person, as strong as the honeyed taste of Scotch that had eased down my throat in the dream. I know, somehow, that Jack is happy.

Wherever he is, I now know that Jack is home free.

Making My Escape

I gave notice to my partners that I will not be staying in the partnership. "I will not sign another lease. I will not be sharing any old or new financial obligations. I will be gone by the end of this December." I gave them five months.

By quitting the partnership I was releasing myself of any financial obligations, which they would interpret as leaving them holding the bag.

They called a meeting to, in effect, cross-examine me – 10 constantly angry men, my remaining partners.

"Jack promised me," I told them.

"What do you mean he promised?" "What did he promise?" "When?" They were doing what cross-examiners do best, erupt with questions. But none of them knew the answer. It's a dangerous thing in this legal game, to ask a question when you don't already know the answer.

"When I went to his house, I told Jack I'd hit a wall. I couldn't litigate anymore. 'Stick with me,' Jack asked. 'Stay with me, with the Bernie case. Until I die. And then,' he promised, 'you can do what the fuck you want.'"

They were all looking down at their hands, at the walls, unable to look at me, the only woman in the partnership, hearing the echo of Jack's voice in their lives, in this, his boardroom. It was Jack being Jack, making me such a promise. There was no way they could hold me, punish me. Jack was gone. The only one who had the authority to contradict me.

"I will be out," I said, "by the end of December, our fiscal year end."

After two-and-a-half hours of their cross-examination of me, inquiring, inquiring into my asset base, my financial viability, I stood up. Afternoon had turned to evening. No one seemed to have seen how the light had changed in the boardroom.

"Gentlemen. I've had enough of this questioning. I've been here for three decades. I have always known this partnership was a *sexless marriage*. I never expected it to end with a *gang bang*."

I closed the boardroom door quietly.

No cake, no lawsuit, either.

When You Get to Where You're Going…

It made the sound of a dog shaking water off its fur. Except it was more like feathers. A big bird ruffling its feathers.

Over my bed. And I thought, *Oh no, a mother bird has nested in my attic. What am I going to do about that, get an exterminator, evict a mother and her chicks in the dead of winter? I can't do that – kick them all out of their nest, even if it happens to be under my roof?*

Again, the rustling. Waiting.

I realize I don't have an attic.

I'm lying there, mulling this over, unwilling to open my eyes, pasted to the bed in the hours between sleep and waking.

And then, *whoomph, whoomph, whoomph, whoomph* as it flaps its huge wings and lifts off and raises itself out through the roof, the sound of its huge wings ever-fainter as it goes.

I open my eyes and look at the ceiling above my face and know: *I have just heard the sound of an angel.*

I want it to be my mother. I want to believe she is telling me that wherever she is, she is finally beyond fear. I'd love to think that she got to see my father again, that she caught up to him in his goneness. I only hear the sound of her wings…her wings beating in free flight.

Small Miracles —a poem by Joyce Carol Oates

After the first death there is a shrinking.
Miracles to fit in a spoon.
The sun rolling free and crazy as the wheel of a baby buggy
      decades old.
The patchwork macaw in the children's zoo dipping
      its oversized beak up and down, up and down,
      merely to amuse.
The God of Trash flinging himself broken to the sidewalk.
The minutes that drain away noisily as we sleep.

Death?—but it was only a piercing, the fleeing
      thread through a needle's eye,
or the shy escape of steam that coalesces
on the first cold surface.

After the first death there is stillness.
The gaps of night between street lamps.
Hard-packed earth that turns to mud, and
      then to earth again, baked by the sun.
After the first death there is a pause.
And then the second death: a pause,
and the third.
This is what we have always known, but forget.

Is each subsequent death easier, one yearns to ask.